DAYS OF SURRENDER

OUR SHADOWS WILL REMAIN

BOOK TWO

ALEC CHARLES

Oxford eBooks

In this series:

Big City Secrets
Days of Surrender
Every Open Eye

PROLOGUE

DOYLE COMES TO see me after I've been inside for almost a whole month. It's such a surprise, being led to the visitors' room without explanation and seeing him sitting there, that I think I'm imagining things… Like a church Father has come to visit a condemned man or something and I've put Doyle's face over his because I'm feeling that lonely, but it really is Doyle. "Doyle," I say as quietly as I can manage once I sit down opposite him.

The visiting area isn't anything like what they show you in the movies; it's just a normal room holding a lot of tables and chairs. Inmates don't sit on opposite sides of reinforced plastic and talk through a telephone; they sit across facing you from the other side of a table with a brightly coloured vest over their shirt. A number of guards walk around at all times - keeping their eyes open to prevent contraband from being handed over.

"How's it going?" he asks reaching across the table and placing a hand over of mine. Nobody bats an eyelid. They must think he's just showing he cares and it's fine because he's a church Father in their eyes. If it wasn't for the off-white dog collar he was wearing, I'd no doubt be marked as a queer for him holding my hand like this.

"Doyle," I say, "they've given me this dipshit of a lawyer who's saying I could get over ten years! The cops are saying my fingerprints matched ones taken from plenty of home and drug store burglaries! Ten years for assault and a couple of robberies," I say in horror. "I'd only be getting a little more than that if I had fucking killed Liefeld's son!"

"Take it easy," Doyle says lighting two cigarettes and of course, it's real easy to say that when you're sitting at his side of the table. "What did they say about bail?" he asks passing me a cigarette.

"You think I'd still be in here if it was that simple? They granted bail," I tell him, "but it's a small fucking fortune because I've got no fixed address. If I pay it," I laugh, "they'd take me straight to a hostel where I'd have cops coming to check up on me throughout the day."

"Fuck," Doyle says, "this is bad."

"But it can get better," I tell him. "You have to get in touch with Tiffany for me. She can afford to pay what they're asking and she can give me a place to stay."

"I don't know…"

"That's because you're not in here," I hiss at him. "I'm serious," I say, "I can't remember her fucking number and I need you to get in touch with her! You think she'll let some asshole lawyer representing me settle for ten years? Fuck," I spit, "she'll have somebody run rings around the prosecution and I'll walk out smiling."

"Are you sure it'd be worth it?" Doyle asks, "In the long run, would it be worth it?"

"Doyle," I grin, "what the fuck are you talking about right now?"

"Think about it," he urges. "If Tiffany really does step up to help you out of this one, she'll be doing it for the publicity."

"And? I don't fucking care," I tell him, "I just want out."

Doyle says, "Then you mustn't have thought it through. She uses you for the publicity," he warns, "and everybody in a worthless little town called Sinclair will find out about it in the newspapers. Whatever it is you had to escape from," he says, "it'll know where you are and how to find you. So tell me," he asks, "is it worth it?"

I want to break down and cry but I don't. I manage to stay strong because no matter how bad it is I'm feeling now, crying in front of everybody will only make it worse for me a little later. I've kept out of trouble for next to a full month. If I break down in tears now, trouble will come looking for me real soon. "Doyle," I say in a hushed voice, "you've got to get me out of here! I can't cope in here!"

"Sure you can," he tries to assure me.

"I can't! Doyle," I tell him, "I'm nothing like you! I'm not tough… I can't look after myself!"

"You can."

"I can't!"

"Lee," he calmly says, "listen to me, would you? Do you want to know what the problem with so many men is? The problem with men like you? It's being scared of hurting somebody. I'm deadly serious," he continues, "it's all that popular talk about not knowing your *real strength*. You think you might come to regret it if you punch somebody and do some real damage. Am I right?" he asks.

"I don't know," I reply.

"You do," Doyle insists. "You know I'm right. All your life, you've been scared of punching somebody that deserves it, just in case they fall down and crack their thick skull open. What you've got to understand," he says, "is this world is filled with people who don't care what damage they cause. You run into one of these people and it doesn't matter whether you have done them no wrong at all and they will try to hurt you as bad as they can. I can't even tell you what they look like or how to tell them apart from anybody else. You could think you're having a heated debate with somebody and the next minute they're trying to take a hold of you. If you stop and think there's a chance they'll see how they're overreacting, you give them the time they need to drive your face into a brick wall. Do you understand what I'm saying?"

"Doyle-"

"What I'm saying is you have a matter of moments to hurt somebody bad enough to stop them from making you hurt even more. Fuck," he says, "what if they were intending to kill you or even worse, cripple you? Don't think about the consequences. Don't think about how you could maybe talk your way out of it.

"An open palm to the nose is always a good opener; even if you don't break it, you have their eyes watering. That second or two you have when they're still blinded? You use that to bring your foot or your knee right between their legs and drop them. Always make a big enough example," he recommends, "so they'll know not to try it again and so will the people who see what you've done or even *hear* about what you've done."

If you're after tales of guys being raped in the showers or even blades hidden in the hollowed-out pages of lengthy tomes so people can be stabbed in the back while they're waiting in the lunch line, I'm afraid I can't help you. My time inside is nothing like the way they make it look out in Hollywood or even on the TV. I saw a couple of fights, but the guards always swooped on in and dragged those responsible out within seconds. And although there were the skinheads with Swastika tattoos always on display and the blacks and the Hispanics and all of these gangs liked nothing more than to glare at one another the fights were nearly always between two guys from the same crew. And as for sex attacks in the shower… If a man is even accused of looking at another man's ass in the showers, his name is dirt and people will spit in his meals walking past his table until somebody else attracts this unwanted attention.

More than anything, I find prison to be boring. The first night the guards gathered a bunch of us together to watch a movie I was a little horrified because it was *A Nightmare on Elm Street* and I was scared the other inmates would be getting ideas but they were fine. I swear, I must have seen every fucking slasher film during my stay. But after seven years of being incarcerated, I'm released.

I'm made to undress in front of a guard and he hands me a box that contains everything I arrived with. I change into my black clothes (they smell real badly of mothballs now) and find an open pack of cigarettes with my Zippo lighter in the pocket. The guard hands me an envelope holding all of the money I've earned by sewing mailbags or screwing mailbox parts together. I thank him and then I'm pushed onto a bus with a number of other inmates due for release - but not before they hand me a letter telling me the address I should make my way to without delay and the address I should head to the next morning to meet my parole officer.

Lighting a cigarette, I fold the letter in half and slip it inside my shirt pocket. It feels good, knowing I'm being released right now, but more than anything else I find myself hoping nobody will try and make conversation with me during the journey.

Figuring I don't have to go straight to the place where I'm

meant to be staying once I'm off the bus, I light another cigarette and purchase a cold bottle of Cherry Coke from a mini-market before making my way to Saint Claire's. But Saint Claire's isn't there waiting for me, and I stand open-mouthed looking at a vacant patch of concrete near tall grass and taller weeds and nettles. "Fuck," I mutter.

A part of me wonders if I could have taken a wrong turn someplace along the way, but I know that isn't the case. I know the wasteland I'm staring at was once my home and now it's gone, all I can do is wonder where Doyle is...

Growing increasingly desperate, I explore the streets Doyle and me used to explore... I stop the people who used to help us out from time to time and ask if they've seen him, but they look at me like I'm a complete stranger and claim to have no idea who I'm talking about. I have to keep walking, resisting the urge to take hold of them and scream how they know full well who it is I'm talking about. The feeling of panic expanding inside my chest gets heavier and heavier. Some of the stores we used to visit have changed their names whereas others are out of business. Los Angeles has changed so much I hardly recognise her and it's making me dizzy and jumpy and I'm exhausted but I'm also wide awake. I finish my cigarettes and immediately buy another pack, taking a combination of long and quick drags on one cigarette after another as if doing so will summon Doyle.

And it works. I find him sitting on the very same wall I was sitting at when I first saw him all those long years ago. The black rucksack I arrived with is even resting at his feet with whatever clothes I had left stuffed into it.

"Doyle," I say, relief washing over me as I approach him. His clothing looks the same as it did last time I saw him, but he looks like shit. He's aged a hell of a lot and he's nothing more than skin and bones. Nothing more than skin and bones and I still can't feel anything other than relief.

"Lee," he says with a warm smile, rising to his feet to embrace me. "It's good they finally let you out."

"Saint Claire's is gone," I say like he wouldn't have known already.

"Yeah," he says in agreement, "they tore it down. But you're out now," he smiles, "at least we have that."

"Yeah," I nod, "at least we have that." I ask if he'd like a cigarette and he says he would, so I hand him one and he lights it with a disposable lighter he takes from one of his pockets. I ask him, "You feel like a drink?"

"Sure," he says with a grin. His dentures are discoloured, a little cracked even. I try to remember if the whites of his eyes were always a little yellow or whether that is also new. "Lead the way," he says. "You are buying, aren't you?"

"Sure," I tell him, "I'm buying," and I bring the black rucksack over my shoulder before we make our way onwards.

I take a couple of bills from the money I was given back at the prison and buy Doyle a bottle of white wine and a bottle of rosé for myself because everything else the store has is pretty expensive. "Pink wine?" Doyle says with a smirk.

"Easiest wine to manage," I say passing him the bottle of white. We walk in almost complete silence, making our way through the park where a man got real angry at me a long time ago for feeding the pigeons. The temperature is starting to drop a little and only a few people are still outdoors. Doyle and I sit at a quiet bench and I take to opening my wine.

"Screw cap?" Doyle grins, watching me.

"I don't know what you find so funny," I smirk. "Your wine is corked. How're you going to open that?" I ask him.

"How do you think?" he smirks, taking a bottle opener from inside his jacket. "Can also be used in a fight," he says, still smiling as he stabs the cork to wind it out from the bottle. "How was prison?" he finally decides to ask.

"Boring," I confess. "It's the whole routine of it all," I explain. "Up at a certain time, washed and fed by a certain time, working until such a time, break for lunch…"

Doyle laughs. "That's how most people live," he says.

"I guess that's true," I say.

I drink a little of my wine. It's not as chilled as I'd like it to be but it's drinkable and that's something.

"You have to stand up for yourself at all?"

"Not once," I tell him.

"You see?" Doyle proudly says, "That's down to the words of advice I gave you. Had people sensing they shouldn't fuck with you."

"Yeah," I sigh, "you're probably right."

"Before I forget," Doyle says reaching into one of his pockets, withdrawing two cigars wrapped in cellophane. "I've been holding onto these," he explains on handing one over, 'especially for today."

"Seriously?" I ask, feeling more than a little touched by it all.

"Seriously," Doyle says as he peels the cellophane back from his cigar. I follow suit. Each of us drops the transparent plastic to the floor, waiting for a strong enough gust of wind to take the waste away from us. We share a flame from Doyle's lighter and we both puff away on our cigars. They taste cheap and a little stale but I figure it's the thought that counts. "To freedom," Doyle says, raising his bottle in a toast.

"And old friends," I add, gently tapping my bottle against his. We sit in silence for a little while, both smiling faintly but not looking at one another. Both taking a draw on our cigar from time to time; both drinking wine from the bottle. We must make quite a sight for the few people still out walking their dogs.

"Have they told you where you've got to stay?" Doyle eventually asks.

"Sure," I tell him.

"Is it far from here?"

"I don't think so," I say. "You could stay there with me... if you want?"

"Nah," he says. "But thanks for the offer."

"It was nothing."

"You're wrong," he says, "that was a good offer." Doyle takes a couple of puffs on his cigar before holding it out in front of his eyes so he can have a good look at it. "This tastes like shit."

"So does the wine," I joke.

"At least the wine takes the taste from your mouth," he says, and he spits to his side before looking back at his cigar. "I can't finish this - I think it's time I quit," he sighs and with that, he flicks it away from him.

"You mind if I copy?"

"Not at all," he grins, so I toss my cigar to one side, happy to know I won't have to go on smoking it. "Guess what?" he asks.

"What?"

"Liefeld and Sons isn't called that these days."

"Really?" I chuckle.

"Really," he says. "It's just called Liefeld's now."

"The old guy retire or die?"

"Maybe both," Doyle says with a shrug.

"You're probably right."

Doyle takes a deep breath, the kind you take when you're trying to buy a little time, trying to decide whether to say one thing or the other, and releases it. "You know Cole and me used to live together?" he finally asks. "Just like me and you."

"I guessed as much," I say with a nod. "I just didn't know if I should ask you to confirm it... Whether it was any of my concern or if it was a sensitive topic for you."

"I wouldn't have minded," Doyle assures me. "But you know," he says, "when you first took to hanging out with Tiffany, I was going to ask you to do me a favour. I was going to ask you to murder Cole for me."

"Get out of here."

"I'm serious," he says, delving a hand into his pocket for a pack of cigarettes. He lights two, hands one to me. I notice the tip is a little pink, like he's got a cut inside his mouth and some blood has gone and found its way onto the filter but I don't mention it. "Cole really upset me," he says like it explains everything, "and I felt betrayed. I was hoping you'd kill him for me and get out of there before the cops got a look at you. Can you imagine how it'd look on Tiffany?" he smirks. "TV star partying with two young men she picked up off the streets..."

"Yeah," I say. "Listen," I ask, "did I piss you off like Cole did?"

"Nah," he says, "I can understand why you went. I never had any bad feelings for you after you left."

"That's good to hear."

"I'm glad you think so. I'm glad everything is looking up for you now," he says and then he takes a breath but he doesn't release it. I look to him, to the smile he's still wearing, and watch the bottle of wine he's holding as it slips from his hands and smashes on the floor.

"Doyle?" I say. "Doyle?"

I take a hold of his wrist. The skin is already as cold as ice.

"Jesus," I softly mutter. "Jesus."

Tears prick at my eyes. I finish my bottle of wine before standing, turning to look at Doyle for one last time. It still looks like he's smiling, it's just that whatever he's smiling at isn't as joyous as it was a couple of minutes ago because the smile is fading. I take a deep breath and try to close his eyelids but they spring back open and it makes me snigger despite myself.

"I'll miss you," I say and I place my empty bottle at his feet. I take another deep breath and pluck the off-white dog collar from his throat before leaving him to be found by the park attendant or whatever. I don't even turn around to see if he's stopped smiling yet; I just walk away knowing it's time for me to leave Los Angeles.

1

All I need is one quick glance and I know the building is empty. Property bought dirt cheap because of the poor economy, apartments within renovated so the owner can charge his tenants an extortionate amount. Tenants paying over the odds in a neighbourhood that probably isn't all that much, just so their struggling neighbours will hear how good they're doing compared to them. Tenants hoping - no, *praying* - a young guy won't break in one night in a desperate attempt to get a little money. Tenants hoping - no, *praying* - that if they're forced to pull the trigger, the intruder will be black.

I walk the block a couple of times before cautiously approaching the building. You know work is being done here during the day but there isn't a sign bearing the name or logo of a security firm in any of the windows. Have things changed so much during my time inside? Do security guards lay in wait now because they pocket a little extra for every derelict they hospitalise?

My second night as a free man and I'm planning on a little breaking and entering.

I spent all of last night and this morning on the road. It turns out people will happily make a stop if the hitchhiker they see is dressed as a man of God. Climb aboard a bus or a train with a small slip of paper in your hand and nobody insists on seeing it up close. They let you get right on and sit down in peace. Some people will even offer you their seat. Smiling to myself at how relatively easy it has been so far, I push all concerns about how I didn't see my parole officer to the back of my mind. I doubt they'll be willing to spend a lot of money searching the USA for me.

Stopping right outside a first floor window of the silent building, I hold a hand over my eyes to get a better look inside the place. It's definitely being renovated; the exposed floorboards are thick with dust and boot-prints, wallpaper has been steamed from the walls and nice looking cupboards still wearing a protective wrap are patiently waiting in the corner of the room. I could do with another day… Just one day to get a look at the place so I have an idea of what time the workmen will arrive in the morning and leave at night, but I don't have a day to spare. I'm exhausted from travelling so far after seven years of being kept in the same area.

I take a deep breath and decide I'll try and open a window. If I'm woken by builders stumbling over me the following morning, I'll probably play at being the holy man with a drink problem and make my exit while they're trying not to laugh too hard in front of me.

"Excuse me?" I hear somebody ask from behind me. I turn, half expecting to see a woman here to deliver her security guard husband's supper to him but see a tiny old lady instead. She looks to the off-white dog collar I'm wearing and smiles. "I thought you were wearing one of those!" she smiles.

"Hello," I say with a nod once it becomes clear to see how she isn't planning on saying anything else, "ma'am. How can I help you?" I ask.

"Oh," she laughs. "It's nothing really," she says, "I was just wondering if you would like a drink – Father…?"

"*Reverend,*" I correct her, and it's not like you can blame me for not having a soft-spot for the term *Father* now, is it? The only real father, the only real family I ever had, was a man from the streets. "Reverend Doyle," I say, offering the old gal a warm smile.

"Oh," she laughs, and the way she keeps laughing that way has me curious to whether she's just a little nervous or trying to flirt with me. "I am sorry," she says, "*Reverend.* But I would like to have a little chat with you and a little drink, if that would be okay?"

"Sure," I shrug. "What have you got to drink?"

"Oh," she says, almost boasting, "I have coffee and decaffeinated coffee, peppermint tea and Darjeeling, herbal and Indian…"

The list just goes on and on and every different type of tea she mentions only acts to make it all the more doubtful she'll have some decent bottles of liquor left to gather dust in the pantry. Once she finally finishes with the tea and moves on to the various fruit juices I interrupt her with a polite enough, "Shall we make our way inside, Mrs…?"

"Miss," she smiles, "Miss Valentino. I live just over the way there."

2

MISS VALENTINO INSISTS we sit at her kitchen table and seeing how my prison cell had much more room to offer than her kitchen, I can only wonder what it is she is trying to hide. The room is so ridiculously cramped that she can't move from one place to the next without having to really *squeeze* past the table I'm sitting at. And then there is the overpowering smell of pine-fresh disinfectant - a smell so strong it almost brings tears to my eyes. Of course, I'm wondering why everything is playing out like this. I'm wondering just what the odds are that Miss Valentino has murdered her romantic partner or whatever and is hoping to make a confession as his body rots away in the adjoining room.

"Here you are," she says on placing a cup down in front of me, "it's Darjeeling, just like you asked for." I've never tried *Darjeeling* tea before. As a matter of fact, I only asked for it because the name sounds a little like *Darling* to me and I thought it was funny.

Valentino turns back around to fix herself a cup of coffee. I notice the photographs slipped within transparent cases, magnetised so they will stick to the refrigerator door. One of them was clearly taken in a nightclub of some kind; a real pretty brunette with a tanned guy resting his head on her shoulder, smiling as he lovingly gazes up at her. I guess the brunette took the picture herself. She really is pretty and I begin to wonder if the guy with the tan is her boyfriend or whether she only sees him as a friend but he's madly in love with her.

I've really no idea how people handle a situation like that. I mean, I was lucky. I was attracted to Eleanor Gayle, I asked if she'd like to go on a date and she said she would. But one of my best friends, a guy named Mark Gainan really liked a cheerleader called Lucy.,, Lucy *Something or Other*, I forget. But Mark didn't have the balls to just ask her if she'd like to see a movie or something, so he befriended her. I'm serious, he was always talking to her and soon he was always meeting her to see a movie or give her a ride someplace, but he never tried to kiss her or anything like that. But then one day, one of our mutual friends threw a party and a small number of us got stupidly high on the prescription painkillers somebody had managed to get a hold of. Mark decided now was the perfect time to tell Lucy how he felt about her so he did and she said she kind of felt the same once but now she only saw him as a friend.

Mark was so distraught by what she said that he killed himself the next day.

I'm sorry, that last bit of information was just a joke. A joke made in poor taste, yes, but still just a joke. Mark was fine when I last saw him, a day or so before leaving Sinclair. He was actually dating Lucy's best friend, the much prettier Karen Paige.

"That's my granddaughter," Miss Valentino says on sitting down with a coffee in her hands and her eyes on me.

"Yes?" I say being snapped away from my own private thoughts and memories. I notice the burgeoning wood I'm currently sporting underneath the table and try not to think about it for fear of it only growing stronger. "Your granddaughter?" I ask. "She's very pretty."

"She is," Miss Valentino nods in agreement. "She's studying Fashion at college. Fashion," she says with a smirk, rolling her eyes in disbelief. "How can you study *Fashion*?" she asks. "They have to design clothing," she explains, "like trousers. Even I know how to draw a pair of trousers, there's nothing to it… I could even colour them in any shade you wanted!"

"There must be a little more to it," I say with a warm smile, solely because I feel like I should be saying something. "Are you expecting her to come and visit tonight?" I inquire- more than a little hopefully.

"Tonight? No," Miss Valentino says. "She stays in Halls during term time. Maybe comes and stays one Saturday out of each month, but that's about it."

"Making the most of her youth." I ask, "Does her boyfriend ever visit with her?" It's probably a sign that I've been kept away from women for too long, but I'm desperate for Miss Valentino to say her granddaughter is single, like I'd then have a chance of bedding her if I happen to bump into her out on the street. I don't even know her name but I'm looking at her captured image up on the refrigerator door and imagining how easy it would be to fall in love with her.

"Boyfriend?" Miss Valentino asks before looking back to the photograph. "Boyfriend!" she laughs. "That isn't her boyfriend," she explains, still laughing, "that's her friend, Buck. Buck is a fag – sorry - queer. Or homosexual. There's *nothing* going on between her and Buck!"

"Well," I say with relief, "they look very happy together." And now that I know what I know, it's hard to look at the guy in the picture, Buck, and not see a queer right away. He's tanned and his hair is styled just right (it even looks to have highlights) and his eyebrows have clearly been plucked recently. Sure, there is a chance he is bisexual, but I try not to think about that possibility.

"Oh," Miss Valentino grins before blowing on her drink, "the stories I could tell you about Buck!" she says. "I'm sorry," she adds, trying not to laugh, "I know I shouldn't gossip like this, especially in front of a reverend."

"Please," I tell her, "we need to know everything you're willing to tell us... How else can we be expected to understand those we encounter?"

3

I WAKE UP in a tiny box-bedroom (even the single-sized bed I'm in must have been difficult to get beyond the door) and wonder where I am for a moment. There's a wooden chair at the end of the bed and the clothes I was wearing have been carefully placed over the back, washed and ironed. It's seeing them that has me remember I'm still at Miss Valentino's ("Call me Ann," she'd insisted) place. She had offered to clean my clothing for me and seeing them has me realise how Miss Valentino must have been up late, first washing and drying them before finally ironing the creases out as best she could.

I stretch and get out of bed to slip into my clothes. There's a framed picture on the wall, sepia coloured to suggest it's real old, of a young boy. And standing beside him, transparent from the knees down, is Jesus Christ himself, like he just couldn't resist jumping into this particular shot.

Pulling up my jeans, I can't help but think over what it was Miss Valentino had really wanted to talk about with me. Father Howard from Miss Valentino's local church was being investigated or something because he was supposedly in a romantic relationship with a young woman called Sophie. Miss Valentino had answered the few questions I had on the matter regarding Howard's age (around forty) and Sophie's age (between thirty and forty). I'd shrugged her concerns away, stating they were both of a respectable age (I stopped myself from cracking wise about a Father not being in a romantic relationship with a young choirboy for a change) and maybe the rumours were nothing more than that. And if it turned out they were? I said we should let God guide them.

Would it really be so bad if a Father was presented with a shot at true happiness? Miss Valentino had said the Bible says you should *not* love anybody more than you love God. I said I couldn't remember that part.

Dressed, I make the bed so it looks like it hasn't been slept in. The sheets are so overly-starched it's any wonder I managed to sleep anyway, and then I step out of the bedroom and make my way down the stairs to the smell of a cooked breakfast. Miss Valentino is at the stove, preparing bacon and eggs and hash-browns and thick sausages and grilled tomatoes with toast. Seeing it all only has me realise how hungry I'm feeling. Only has me realise I haven't eaten a breakfast this good since… since I was living with Tiffany Lily. "You're up," Miss Valentino smiles on noticing me. "I was going to bring this up to your room. Take a seat," she says.

"Thanks," I say pulling out a chair. "Is there anything I can do?" I ask, hoping she'll refuse all offers of assistance.

"You can tell me how you take your coffee," she replies and I tell her I have it black and with one sugar. One sugar sounds so respectable, doesn't it?

We eat breakfast together. Miss Valentino says as if to remind me, "When I first saw you yesterday, a part of me thought you must be here to investigate Father Howard."

"Not me," I smile back at her.

"So where is it you're going?" she asks.

"I don't know," I tell her. "The Lord urged me to walk and so that's what I'm doing."

"Do you really have no idea where it is you're going?"

"Not yet," I say. "But sometimes you just have to do what you're being told to do."

"Of course. But where are you from?" she wants to know. "I mean, where was your church?"

"Originally," I answer, "I'm from a small town far from here called Sinclair. Have you ever heard of the place?"

"I don't think I have," she says. Hallelujah.

"Not many people have," I tell her. "I think the only people who know it exists are the people that reside there. But for a while," I finish, "I was in Los Angeles."

"Los Angeles," she says. "So you haven't travelled too far… Not recently, I mean."

"Only in spirit," I reply, and she smiles on hearing that one.

"Do you think you'll ever return to Los Angeles?"

"It's doubtful," I say. "Everything I could do there has been done."

"What about Sinclair? Do you think you'll ever return home?" she asks.

"I don't know," I tell her. "I doubt it, but you never can tell. A few years back," I confess, "I'd have told you I'd never return to Sinclair."

Miss Valentino nods like she knows exactly what it is I'm talking about.

When I'm leaving, she thrusts thirty dollars into my hand and I tell her I can't take it.

"Please," she says, "it's only money I would have given to the church if I hadn't stopped attending."

"How have you been feeling," I ask her, "since you stopped attending Father Howard's sermons?"

"I don't know," she says. "At first I thought I was angry at him."

"And now?"

"Now I'm not too sure about what I should be feeling."

"You should go on Sunday," I say, holding the thirty dollars out for her to reclaim.

"I will," she says closing my fingers around the money, "but I still want you to have that."

I thank her, pocket the money and walk away.

4

I'M JUST ABOUT to walk on into the train station when I hear a woman call out, "Hey!" I look to my side and see her standing beside her car and now that I'm looking at her she grins and shrugs her shoulders before asking, "What's the matter, are you deaf? I called you two times already." I turn, intending to walk towards her, and her eyes fall onto my off-white dog collar and a look of shame possesses her soft features. "Oh," she says, "I'm sorry, I didn't know you were a Father."

"I'm not," I say, walking to her. "I'm a reverend."

"Same thing," she asks, "right? I'm sorry," she immediately adds, "that was a joke. I'm always cracking jokes, it's just that they're never the funny kind."

"Keep at it," I say, "and you'll get there in the end. But what is it you want? Are you having car trouble or something?"

"Something," she smirks. "I'm in a real tight jam," she explains, turning to pop the hood, "so I'm hoping to find somebody who's willing to buy *something*."

Looking at all the available junk, I'm transported back to Sinclair. I'm back to the day when I bought Crowley's Book of Thoth from some stranger down on his luck but this time, I can refuse it if I really want to.

"Well?" she asks, bringing me back to the here and now. "Do you see anything you like?"

"I doubt it," I say but I ease my hand over the pile of trash she's trying to rid herself of. I push aside things that have no real interest to me but could probably be sold on to somebody else at a higher price, it's just that she doesn't have the time. I smile, unearthing a Bible and hold it up for her to see. "I think you might need this," I grin.

"No thank you," she smirks. "You don't have the slightest idea of the trouble *that* book has gotten me into."

"Right," I say, flicking through the pages. "Why don't you just toss it or, even yet, burn it?"

"I'm not doing that," she says, "I could get all kinds of bad luck if I do. But what do you think, you want to buy a Bible? Good as new, never been read."

"That's funny," I chuckle. "How much do you want for it?"

She asks, "Are you serious? I mean, you're a reverend."

"I left my copy at home," I say, dropping a hand into my pocket. "How much?"

"I don't know," she says. "How much are you willing to pay for it?"

I turn a little so she can't see how much I'm holding and I carefully ease out a five before tucking the rest deep inside my pocket. "Five dollars?" I ask.

"You're the man of God," she says, stepping forward to quickly take the money from me before I have a chance to reconsider, 'you should know better than me how much the word of God should set you back."

"Yeah," I grin, taking the cigarettes and Zippo lighter from my jacket. "I guess I should."

"Could I bum a smoke?" she asks, eyes on the cigarette pack I'm holding. "I left mine at home," she adds.

"Sure," I tell her and I hand her a cigarette. I light my cigarette before handing her the lighter.

"Thanks," she says and once she's lighted up and is handing it back she adds, "you can't smoke inside the station," like she's trying to be friendly or something.

"Thanks for letting me know," I tell her. "Looks like we're together for a couple more minutes."

"Good," she says, "people might think I'm collecting for the church. Sorry, that was a bad joke."

"It wasn't too bad," I tell her.

She coughs a little, like maybe she isn't a real smoker, but I act like I didn't notice. "So what's your name, anyway?" she asks. "Reverend…?"

"Doyle," I reply. "Reverend Doyle."

"Are you from here?"

"No," I say, "are you?"

"Not originally," she says, "and I'm looking to move on."

"That's what I'm doing myself." I ask her, "Do you know where it is you're headed?"

"I don't know," she says. Maybe California, someplace like that."

"Stay clear of Los Angeles," I advise.

"Sure," she nods, "but how come?"

"It's not the best place to be if you don't know anybody, and there's nobody there to help you. Not anymore."

She nods as if in understanding and takes a slow drag on her cigarette. "Thanks for the advice," she says.

"Don't sweat it," I tell her. "But what's your name, anyway? That's if you don't mind my asking…"

"I don't mind," she laughs, "and you gave me yours, so fair's fair. It's Naomi," she says.

"Naomi," I say with a nod. "It's not a particularly common name."

"Maybe," she says, "but when I was at school, my best friend was called Fuchsia."

I ask, "Like the plant?"

"Like the plant," she laughs. "When she got a little older, she asked us to all call her by her middle name."

"What was that," I ask, "Rose?"

"That's almost as bad as one of mine," she laughs. "But no," she continues, "her middle name was Lauren."

"Like Bacall?"

"Sure," she says, "like Bacall."

"Well," I say with a smile, "I once read that's not even her real name."

5

I STEP OFF the train after three, maybe four stops because it dawns on me that it would probably be a much better idea to travel during the night so I can guarantee myself just a little sleep. The town I'm in looks a lot like TV producers will make towns look to give a quaint, homely feel. The towns I went through before stepping off the train looked almost identical to it. Because that is what happens once you're travelling *away* from the major cities; everything turns small and empty until you're headed *toward* the big cities again and then everything turns big and flash.

Despite the rucksack I'm carrying over my shoulder, people are only all too happy to smile and be polite to me and I put that down to the off-white dog collar I'm wearing. If it wasn't for the dog-collar, the local lawmen probably would have turned up by now to insist I accept their offer of a ride out of town. I light a cigarette and smile back at everybody who smiles at me, and I mention how wonderful the weather is and trivial things like that before stepping inside a small diner for a cup of coffee.

The waitress brings my order over with the day's newspaper and I notice the tattoo on her ring finger as she does. A small tattoo of a heart, the only colour being the black of the thick outline. "The paper's mine," she explains, "and I was going to read it during my break, but you can read it while you're here."

"Thanks," I say to her, "I'll remember to hand it back before I leave."

The waitress smiles and turns away. I watch her heading back to the counter because she is pretty good looking, the kind of young blonde waitress all the regulars here are probably hitting on every day. And again I find myself wondering if I'd have been granted such an act of kindness like this if it wasn't for the collar around my neck. I swallow and gently run a finger across the collar, remembering Doyle. I wonder how badly his body was treated once it was shoved into the back of a van and carried over to the nearest hospital. The collar would have seen him being treated with some dignity, but I went and claimed it as my own like a bastard.

I read the newspaper to take my mind off things. There's talk of a Republican senator called *Rhea* making it clear for all to see that he wants to stand for president as soon as he can. The article gives a list of things the politician has recently done just to appear on TV and in print he looks like a good guy you could rely on to run the country. When it mentions his strict, religious upbringing, I sigh and turn the page. Realising my coffee is only lukewarm at best I drink it down before closing and folding the newspaper neatly in half, then carry both it and the empty cup over to the counter. The same waitress looks up at me from the dishes she is busy washing and smiles. "I'm sorry," she says, "I didn't see you there."

"It's okay," I tell her, "I'm just returning the newspaper and the cup."

"Thanks," she says. "Aren't you just the sweetest?"

"I don't know about that," I laugh and I look to her blouse in search of a nametag but she isn't wearing one. "If you don't mind my asking," I say, "what's your name?"

"My name?" She smiles and says, "I'm Abigail," and she removes her hand from the sink filled with soapy water and holds it out for me to take. I laugh, accepting it. Her skin feels a lot warmer than it should.

"It's a pleasure to meet you," I say, "Abigail. I'm Reverend Doyle."

"Reverend Doyle," she says back to me. "It was a pleasure to meet you."

"Thank you," I grin. "Say, could you tell me of any good places to go nearby?"

"What kind of places?" Abigail asks, "You want the kind of places to kill a little time or are you looking for a place to stay?"

"I don't know," I shrug. "Both," I say, "maybe."

Abigail nods; looks up at the ceiling for a moment and then back at me. "You walk out of here and turn left," she says, "and you keep walking down that road and it'll take you to the heart of the town. *Everything* is easy to find from there," she says, "motels, movie theatres, even bars if you're inclined to drink."

"Of course I drink," I desperately joke, "Jesus encouraged it. But what about you," I ask, "you go out much around here?"

"I don't know," she says, "maybe every once in a while."

"To the nearby bars you just mentioned?"

"Sure," she smiles.

I ask her, "What time do you finish?"

"Seven," she says.

"Seven," I repeat with a nod. "And what's your favourite bar near here?"

"My favourite?" she laughs. "I don't know... McFarlanes' Bar and Grill," she says.

"And that place is easy to find?"

"Yeah," she laughs.

"What do you think the chances are," I say, "of me being in McFarlanes' Bar and Grill and you turning up at around ten-after-seven?"

"I don't know," she says, "I have to tidy the place before I can leave. But around fifteen-after-seven," she blushes, looking back down at the dishes she'd clean forgotten about, "I could be there around then."

"That's good," I say, "in fact, it's great. You can show me all the sights this town has to offer."

"Sure," she says, "that would be cool."

"Cool," I say and I turn for the exit and add, "so I'll maybe see you later. Wait," I ask, turning back around, "what's the name of this town, anyway?"

"Are you serious?" she laughs.

"Sure," I chuckle. "Where am I right now?"

"McFarlanes," she says. "You're in McFarlanes."

"Thanks," I tell her, "I'll see you later," I leave the diner and immediately turn left, lighting up a cigarette. The sun is shining so brightly that I can feel the hot sidewalk through the soles of my shoes. The sun itself seems to be trying to tear clean through the back of my jacket to set my shirt alight but I keep my jacket on and keep walking, trying to convince myself that the noticeably cleaner air is reason enough to stay in a place like McFarlanes.

Eventually, the road becomes a whole lot wider and it happens so gradually that you don't even notice it to begin with. But I'm clearly in the heart of town. I spot McFarlanes' Bar and Grill make my way over to the establishment. Blinds long bleached a shade of ivory by the sun are behind the glass windows, open yet showing nothing but darkness within. I push the oak door open regardless and step on inside the place. It's cool, dark and almost completely deserted. A real old man is sitting on a stool behind the bar, already looking over at me. He's wearing a trucker's cap, steel-rimmed spectacles and a faded orange T-shirt under blue dungarees.

6

I'm standing right in front of the counter and I'm looking over at the collection of bottled beers and the different labels on the taps. The old man gets up from his stool really slow and takes even slower steps toward me with his hands on his hips. Once he's close enough, you can see how thick his eyeglasses are. You wonder if maybe if keeps his bar so dark just to prevent you from seeing how large his eyes appear to be. "Hey," he says quietly and it sounds more like a disgruntled 'Huh.' "What can I get you?" he asks.

"This beer here," I ask on pointing at one of the taps seeing how it has McFARLANES' BEST written over it, "this made here?"

"Yep," the barman says reaching up over the bar to pull a clean glass down from the shelf, "made in town. McFarlanes' local beer."

"Is it any good?" I ask him like there's even the slightest chance he'd answer truthfully if it wasn't.

"They don't call it *Best* for nothing," he smiles, paying more attention to the glass he's now filling from the tap than he is to me. McFarlanes' Best is golden-honey in colour and the foamy head is whiter than the purest of snow.

"I'll tell you what," I say with a smile, "I'll have me a glass of that."

I slip my hand into my pocket but the barman doesn't seem to be paying me any attention. He just fills the glass and then he lifts it to the bar, sweeping a little excess foam from the top using something that looks a lot like a knife. "Here you go," he says on pushing the glass over to me.

"Thanks," I tell him. "How much do I owe you?"

"Nothing," he says with a wave of his hand, making his way back to his stool. "Drink's on me," he says sitting down, "seeing that you're a preacher."

"Thank you," I say. I look at the drink with hungry eyes, savouring the very sight and smell of it before daring to partake of it. And I think about Doyle again and wonder how he would have reacted to such a kind offer. He probably would have settled down in McFarlanes and left Los Angeles in his past if he even believed for one moment he could get his drinking done for free and without having to do any lifting.

"To McFarlanes," I say raising my glass but the barman doesn't hear me or simply acts like he doesn't. I bring the glass to my mouth, trying to ignore the foam which I have always hated and drink a little down. It's cold but a little too fizzy; maybe a little too gassy. It tastes just like most any other kind of beer you can buy. But I have to admit, the colour of it is real nice.

"This just might be the best drink I've ever had," I call out to the barman a little louder but he carries on ignoring me. Seeing how I'm not getting any conversation, I slip a hand into my pocket and pull out the open pack of cigarettes and Zippo lighter. It's only once I've got a cigarette out of the pack that I realise you may not be allowed to smoke here. "Damn," I say before calling out a little louder still, "hey- can you smoke in here?"

The barman slowly turns his head to look at me. "There are no signs saying you can't," he says.

"I know," I tell him, "but I've been away, travelling," I claim, "for the last couple of years and now all of a sudden, it seems like we have different smoking laws for different areas. So," I shrug before asking for the second time, "are you allowed to smoke in here?"

"Are you a man of God?"

"Sure," I lie.

"Then you're allowed to smoke in here," the barman says, looking away from me as soon as he can. Man seems to love nothing more than to stare at his feet. I light a cigarette, pull the smoke deep inside my lungs and take to looking around the bar. I notice a framed picture of The Beatles right above the door. I'm guessing it was taken in the late 60s; they've got the long hair but are clean shaven. John seems to be leading the way and Paul is right behind him. Whereas all the others are looking straight ahead and determined, Paul's head seems a little bowed, like he's feeling sad about something. I wonder what it could be making him feel that way for a moment before reminding myself just how long ago that the picture was taken exactly. You could probably send a copy of it to Sir Paul himself and he would have no recollection of it. The Beatles must have been photographed more times than anybody else in the world. More times than the Virgin Mary has appeared in a patch of spilled oil.

"Say," I call out to the barman, "who was your favourite Beatle?"

The barman doesn't look to me but he shrugs and says just loud enough for me to hear, "Can't say I ever liked them enough to have a favourite."

"Mine's George," I say anyway. "My brother always preferred Paul. He thought almost everything Paul did up to a point was just fantastic."

The barman goes on like he hasn't heard my last bit of information but I don't bother repeating it, I just glance back over to the picture above the door. Every bit of knowledge I have on The Beatles was handed down to me by my mom, who had absolutely loved them. I can still remember a lot of the clues on the sleeves… clues that Paul had died in a road accident and been replaced by a lookalike. Clues that are still denied to this day because admitting that they're there would be like admitting you maybe played a part in driving Charles Manson crazy. And the part in Hey Jude where Lennon can be heard saying 'Fucking hell!' in the background, apparently because his headphones slipped off. Mom told me that at some point or another, every one of The Beatles had been a bit of an asshole. Well, every one of The Beatles apart from Ringo.

And then there was my older brother, who spent one summer trying to learn how to play bass guitar, like he thought playing bass would maybe make him Paul McCartney.

I finish my drink, thank the barman and leave. Maybe if somebody else had been in here, anybody else, I'd have been happy to down another beer, but having an old and silent barman for company is far from thrilling.

7

I SMOKE A cigarette and get up from the wooden bench in the heart of McFarlanes and I spread my jacket out on the floor in front of me before taking the Bible from my rucksack. I flick through a number of pages, not wanting to start too near the beginning, and then I take to reading out the printed words for all to hear. I want to see if I can encourage people to hand their money over like Doyle could but I have to stop once I start condoning the rape of your enemy's daughters. Seriously, that's in the Bible. I can't fucking believe what I'm reading… can't believe how people can even dare claim the Bible is a book of love and understanding. I guess people who say the Bible is a real nice book simply haven't read it. Or not all of it, anyway. Maybe they've just attended church on the occasional Sunday morning and the priest has read something nice and cheerful for them all to hear. The priest sends his people forward to spread the word but they have no idea to what the word really is.

So I close the book and return it to the safety of my rucksack before lighting another cigarette to gather my thoughts. A couple of people still insist on dropping loose change onto my jacket, like they're paying for my silence. It's understandable, especially after some of the shit I've just been spouting. But then Doyle comes to mind and I remember parts of the sermon he gave about some of the shit that has gone down in the Middle East… How only an *Old Testament God* could ever agree with that and I finally understand what he had meant. The words seem heavy with truth now. They could even be important. So I take a deep breath, toss my cigarette into the gutter and clear my throat before I start preaching about how wrong it is for US politicians to be saying they're guided by Jesus as they're doing stuff out in the Middle East that only an Old Testament God could ever agree with.

And people take to looking at me as they walk on by. Some of them even stop to listen.

And I'm just pulling all this clean out of my ass. I'm tripping over my words and repeating myself as I desperately try to remember how Doyle had put it but I'm saying one part as I remember the part I should have said first, so it's a mess but I'm speaking with such passion and belief that I can't stop myself. I feel like I could actually be making a difference here, if just *one* person hears what it is I'm saying and passes the words along. They're not my words, but…

"Hey!" somebody yells from the side of me. The guy responsible for cutting me off is ugly with an upturned nose and he's wearing braces. His skin is showing the first signs of sunburn and his shoulders are huge, just like his arms. "My brother's best friend was shot by one of them sand niggers!" he shouts right before he punches me in the mouth. A lot of people gasp as I fall back onto my ass. Some people who had been walking by stop to take a look at what will happen next, but nobody even tries to intervene. They want to see it all play out naturally.

"Yeah," the ugly guy says with his eyes locked onto me, "yeah you take that!" he says. "Come on," he says, "come on and get up so I can kick your stupid ass back down!"

There's a copper-like taste in my mouth. I raise a finger to my lips and immediately pull it back on feeling a sharp pain. A drop of blood is on the end of my finger because the asshole busted my bottom lip open when he punched me.

"Come on," he continues, "come on and get up!" he says. More people have stopped to watch events unfold now. More than *anything* I want to get to my feet, drive an open palm into the ugly guy's nose and then kick him in the crotch before finally stomping on his face as he's writhing around at my feet. "Yeah," he smiles as I pull myself up, "let's see what you got, you commie! You flag burner! You-"

I look at him and I turn my other cheek to him. I don't put up any form of guard or attack. I just offer him my cheek. He quickly takes a step forward and makes out like he's about to hit me but he doesn't and I don't flinch anyway. It's the fact I didn't flinch that leaves him looking stupid. "Wayne!" a young girl shouts, pushing her way to the front. "What are you doing, fighting with a man of God?!"

"You didn't hear what he was saying," he whimpers to her. "You didn't hear-"

She slaps him hard across the face and storms off. 'Wayne' rubs at the skin where she had hit him before chasing after her without giving me a second look. Slowly but surely, the people who had gathered to watch turn and head in their own directions. Some of them look a little ashamed at how they didn't get involved. A sweet-looking old girl who smells of mints comes over to me, lets me know what a wonderful thing she thinks I just did.

"It was nothing," I say, lifting my coat from the ground before walking on. Abigail will arrive at McFarlanes' Bar and Grill to find an empty stool, that's if she was intending to meet me at all. By seven-fifteen, I'll be long out of this town, walking on again. I remind myself how I finished things with Eleanor before they had a chance to go wrong. Leaving Abigail like this is just the same.

8

I TRAVEL FOR the best part of two days and three nights and I don't lose the small towns because I don't head in a straight line; I jump on buses or coaches and trains to keep me going in a mixture of directions. And it's morning when I wake up as the latest train is stopping in another small town. I get to see the town is called Whicker and, just for the hell of it, I get up from my seat and grab my rucksack to jump off before the train starts moving again. Even in my rush to the exit, I manage to grab some stranger's wallet from his pocket. He probably won't notice it's gone until he gets off the train someplace down the line.

Again, the air is noticeably fresh and I wonder if maybe Los Angeles just has the misfortune of heavily polluted air. A couple of kids rush by me on scooters. One of them, a boy with strawberry blond hair beneath a dark red baseball cap, looks back over his shoulder to say, "Hello," to me. I return the greeting but I doubt he hears it. He's already pretty far ahead.

I head down the stone steps of the station and just get to walking. Something tells me that I'll be staying in Whicker for a while but I can't tell you why. I go by a pub but it's closed. The diner a couple of doors down is open, so I head inside. It's a little crowded but everybody inside is already drinking their coffee and eating their breakfast, so I'm served almost immediately. The waitress smiles at me as she hands me the coffee I've ordered and asks, "You here to try and steal the reverend's job?"

"Just checking out the competition," I joke.

"You don't have far to go," she laughs. "Church is just around the corner."

"Thank you," I say. She turns and walks away. I look around but can't find a newspaper anybody has left behind so I'm left with only my thoughts and I don't like the idea of being left alone with those for too long. "Excuse me?" I call out to the waitress.

"Yes?" she says.

I ask her, "Are you allowed to smoke in here?"

"I'm afraid not," she says. "Not anymore. But you can step outside and have a smoke and I won't take away your drink."

"It's okay," I tell her, "but thanks."

I'm not hungry but I don't want to unexpectedly find myself feeling hungry so I ask for another coffee because Tiffany once told me coffee is a hunger suppressant. Or maybe it was Doyle who told me that. I take my time with the second cup and I keep looking around, waiting for somebody to leave a newspaper behind but nobody does. In the end I just finish my drink and ask the waitress, "Where'd you say the church was?"

"Turn right when you walk out of here," she says, "walk straight on up the road and take the first left. You can't miss it."

"Thanks," I say, intending to spend some time looking at the local church. I can't remember stepping inside of one since a number of them rejected me back in Los Angeles, but I figure things have to be different in small towns like this one, even if it's only the architecture.

"What's your name, anyway?" the waitress wants to know.

"Reverend Doyle," I tell her.

"Well," she says, "it was a pleasure to meet you and I look forward to seeing you again."

"Likewise," I say, getting to my feet.

"One word of warning," she adds with a giggle, "if you're hoping to catch the reverend's morning sermon; try to *sneak* in. I swear," she laughs, shaking her head, "he can point you out in front of everybody when you arrive late and he makes a couple of jokes at your expense."

I say, "Thanks for the warning," and then I leave. I turn right and walk straight up the road until I can make a left and I see the church right away. Big but pretty cosy-looking. Lighting a cigarette, I walk by with plans of going straight past and returning once the sermon has had enough time to end but I stop, noticing how the name of the local reverend is on a board out front. REVEREND LEESON is spelled out in white, block letters and it makes me smirk. Leeson only has me think *Lee Son* or maybe even *Lee's Son* if you really push at it. It's a name I could have just as easily taken.

"What the heck," I smirk, dropping my smoke beside me as I make way to the door. I step inside and find the place to be real cool and pretty full. There's room for me to sit on a pew at the back so I immediately take it, determined not to become the butt of Leeson's gag about even holy men being late for church these days, and an old lady looks to my dog-collar with excitement and mouths something I don't make out. I smile back at her and then look up to the front, up at Leeson, for the first time. He's wearing cream slacks and a pale blue shirt with an open collar. He's giving a pretty light-hearted sermon, walking up and down making jokes instead of remaining behind the podium up at the altar with an open Bible in front of him. He's also my older brother.

9

He finishes his sermon and I rush outside to light up a cigarette. Instead of standing right by the door, I make my way back to the road. I don't want him to walk out and right into my path, I want to hang around unnoticed and get a real good look at him. It's funny; I'd watched his entire performance and known without shadow of a doubt that *Reverend Leeson* was my older brother, but now… but now…

It can't be possible. It has to be a mistake of some sort. Like maybe I'm still tired or the heat is too much or I haven't been eating enough or all three. Cold sweat trickles down my spine. I drag smoke deep inside my lungs as the worshippers slowly take to coming out into the sun, starting with the old gals I was sitting beside. Like me, they don't wait around outside to shake his hand or anything, they come walking right for the road. They take the time to stop in front of me and one of them asks, "What did you think of Reverend Leeson?"

"Yeah," I say, "he was real good… Real inspirational."

"I wasn't sure about him when he first took over from Reverend Mills," the other says in the strictest of confidence, "but his manner has kept people coming."

"How long ago was that?" I ask her.

"How long ago was *what*?" she says, looking a little confused.

"That he took over."

"Five," she says to her friend, "six years?"

"Yes," her friend says in agreement, "something like that."

"And that's when Reverend Leeson first arrived here?"

"Oh no," one of the two ladies says with a smile. "I remember when he first arrived in town. That must have been… I don't know, around twenty years. Yes," she decides, "he must have arrived near twenty years ago and was residing with Reverend Mills almost right away."

"And he was always a reverend?"

"Well," she says, "he was always wearing the collar back then." A car eases to a stop behind me and the driver gently taps his horn. "That's our lift back to the home," she says to me, both gals stepping by to reach the car. "It was a pleasure to meet you, Mr…?"

"Doyle," I say watching the church doors, people still coming out of them. "Reverend Doyle."

Few people seem interested in hanging around to talk with the good reverend, who is yet to venture out into the morning sun. They walk by me, all smiles and greetings. I return the smiles without taking my eyes from the door. I don't even try and talk them into donating a little money like Doyle would have done, because I'm scared doing so will have me miss the good reverend.

A beautiful girl of around seventeen or eighteen, a real looker with tits that don't look too big but would be a decent handful, heads in my direction with a friendly smile but I don't pay it too much attention because everybody else is doing the same. Even when she comes to a stop to the side of me, I carry on looking right at the door. "Good morning," she says to me.

"Good morning," I say and I drop my cigarette before stepping down on it. I immediately regret doing that, figuring no man of God would drop a cigarette stub on sacred ground, but don't focus on it for too long. I just light another cigarette and keep my eyes open for Leeson.

"Are you waiting to speak with Reverend Leeson?" she asks.

"I sure am. Nothing too important," I decide to add.

"Is he expecting you?"

"I don't think so." Just to be polite and to try and speed things along I ask her, "You want a smoke?"

"No," she laughs, "I don't smoke. But thanks."

"Smart choice."

The girl asks, "What do you mean?"

"Not smoking," I tell her. "I get no pleasure out of it… It's just a bad habit. Like biting your nails or something as dirty."

She laughs again. "A teacher told me that biting your nails is as hygienic as licking a toilet bowl," she says.

"I don't know if I believe that," I tell her without looking away from the door for even a second. "And how dirty a toilet are we talking?"

"I don't know," she laughs again. "I'm Maria."

"I'm Reverend Doyle."

A beautiful woman is next out, chatting alongside an old man who says goodbye to her and hangs back at the door for Leeson's imminent arrival. Maria holds a hand in the air and calls out, "Mom!" to the beautiful woman. The beautiful woman looks up and waves back to her daughter, eyeing me with a little suspicion as she heads over to us. "That's my mom," Maria informs me. I bite my tongue instead of saying something like, "I'd never have guessed." But even looking past the beautiful woman for fear of missing Leeson, a part of me thinks she looks a little too young to be the girl's mother.

"Hi," she says to me, placing a protective arm around her daughter's shoulders.

"Hi," I say back to her.

"I've never seen you in town before," she says.

"I'm new in town," I tell her and, hoping to stop people from talking about me too much, I offer her my hand and say, "I'm Reverend Doyle."

"It's a pleasure to meet you," she says. "I'm Laura and this is my daughter, Maria." She gives me time to say something before speaking again. "Are you waiting for Paul?"

I turn to her and try not to smile, hearing the name he has chosen. "Paul?" I ask.

"Reverend Leeson." She says, "My husband, and this little one's father."

I look to Maria and back to Laura. "She's too old to be his daughter, isn't she?" I ask despite myself. Maria laughs at that. Laura playfully nudges her daughter in the side before looking back at me with a smile.

"Maria is only fifteen," she says.

"Fifteen," I mutter. I do a couple of calculations in my head, figure it's possible. It would mean something like two years after he'd abandoned me he had settled down and started his own happy family without giving me a second thought, but that's believable. His happily getting on with his life and not giving a fuck about me, I mean. "Wow," I say, just to try and get a little more information without making her too suspicious, "I'd never have thought you were old enough to have a fifteen year old daughter. It's hard to imagine you could have been married for twenty years."

"He's a charmer," Laura says to her daughter, "no wonder you're happy talking with him. Not twenty years," she says to me with a smile, "nearly, but not twenty."

Leeson finally comes out of the doors, all smiles as he stops to talk with those who have been patiently waiting for him. Maria says, "Here's dad."

Laura looks over to her husband and smiles. "Almost twenty years," she says. "That's hard even for me to believe," she reveals. "I still remember the day he first arrived here."

10

Leeson finally shakes hands with the last person and then he turns and spots us. Well, he spots me standing with his family. There's a smile on his face, aimed at the wife and daughter, obviously but even from where I'm standing I can tell it's a troubled smile. Even his eyes give away his feelings; they're a little funny, like maybe the sun is a little too bright behind me, but it's more than that. I know it's more than that, just like I know he's my brother even from where he's standing.

He starts walking over to us, pretty slowly like he wants to get a good look at me. I wonder if he recognises me but just isn't sure from where or when. Because I'm starting to tremble as he carries on heading over, I take the pack of cigarettes from my pocket and light up. I offer the pack to Laura and ask her, "Would you like a cigarette?"

"No," she says with a wave of her hand, "but thank you. I quit the minute Maria was expected."

"That's real good of you," I say before blowing smoke from the corner of my mouth.

He finally reaches us and he smiles in Maria's general direction and then he takes a hold of Laura's hand but not once does he stop looking at me. Up close, the look in his eyes is impossible to ignore. I don't doubt for one second that he's struggling to remember just how it is he knows me. And that's only all too understandable. He walked out before puberty had even kicked in for me. A few years back, I also had my nose broken pretty bad. Then there are the other things, like prison and everything else. Things like that change how you see the world and even that can dramatically change how you appear to others.

"Hi," he says to me, "I see you've already met my family. I'm Reverend Leeson."

"You've a wonderful family," I smile, offering him my hand, "I'm Reverend Doyle."

We shake hands. Briefly, but he tries to look right through me. I can see how it's troubling him, my being here, and I wonder if his wife or daughter has noticed it yet.

"I caught your sermon," I say, still smiling. "The number of worshippers you had in there was just as impressive."

"Thank you," he says. "I'm sorry," he finally decides to ask, "but have we ever met before?"

"Oh," I grin, "I don't think so. Maybe in spirit," I say, touching the dog collar around my throat, "what with us being brothers. But I don't think we've ever met before, Leeson."

He smiles and shrugs his shoulders, saying, "I just thought I'd check. But what can I do you for?" he wants to know. "Have you been sent here for any reason?"

"Oh," I laugh, "I hope I haven't had you worrying! No," I tell him, "I haven't been sent here to check up on you or anything like that. I'm just travelling up north," I claim, "and I took an extra week's vacation so I can have a little time to relax to myself before I reach where it is I'm headed. I only caught you at work," I finish, "completely by chance. I just thought it would be polite to stop and say hello, what with us being of the one father."

"Oh, he says and you can see the tension drop from him right away. He allows the important things to pass him by unnoticed and that has me wondering if I was the same, back when I was with Tiffany Lily. Once you no longer have to struggle to survive, you turn weak and stupid. I can't help but wonder what it will take for his instincts to be kicked back into touch.

"That's very kind of you," he says. "I'm glad you enjoyed what you saw. You say you're travelling north?"

"That's right," I nod. "I'll stay here a week," I say, "maybe a little longer. It all depends."

"Have you got a place to stay?"

"No," I reply, wondering if he's about to offer me his spare room or something.

"Well," he says, "you could do a lot worse than the Four Card motel over on Central Street. Just be sure to tell Mitch that I sent you," he grins.

"Thanks," I tell him. "I will."

Maria suddenly asks me, "What are you doing now?" and before I have a chance to answer her she says, "We're about to go and get some waffles if you'd like to come with us?"

"Maria!" Laura laughs. "He could have to meet friends or family and now you'll have him thinking it'll look rude if he doesn't come with us!"

"No offence caused," I smile, dropping my cigarette to the floor. "But like I already said- right now is my time. I'd love nothing more than to join you for waffles. I'm sure you could tell me the best places to visit," I add looking to Leeson, "maybe even talk about what is was exactly that had you decide to settle here?"

11

We don't head to the diner I've already been to but a place called Waldo's Waffles. Walking into the place, I try to figure how the four of us must look, a group of friends or a happy family? And I realise that's what we are… a family. Paul Leeson is/was my older brother. That means his wife, Laura, is my sister in law and their daughter, Maria, is my niece. It's Maria who leads the way, followed by her mother and then me. Being the gentleman, Leeson follows from the back and holds the door open for me. I thank him with a knowing grin he seems unable to read.

"So," I ask as we make our way to a table for four, "do you come here every Sunday?"

Maria slips into one of the red leather wall chairs and Laura takes the one beside her, meaning Leeson and I will have to sit next to one another. I realise he's not with us right now but at the counter, talking with a young waitress. "Not every Sunday," Maria says to answer my question, "only when it's a nice day so we're not in the car."

"Paul would have us walking everywhere, every day," Laura laughs, "come rain or shine!" I notice, not for the first time, that she's a little more than pretty. She's a lay you would brag about to your friends even if you weren't that kind of guy. And I can't help but think about how good it would make me feel if I fucked her. I'm not even saying Leeson would have to know what I had done; it could possibly be enough just for me to know. And Laura would *have* to be up for it, surely?

The small-town Reverend's Wife with a teenage daughter… Laura and the rev' were probably sleeping in separate beds already. Leeson was no doubt a good father, helping Maria with her homework and school projects, but he was most likely impotent. Suddenly afraid of sex at the very least… staying in his den until he was sure Laura would be asleep (or at least willing to pretend she was). Next morning he makes excuses about how he was preparing a complex sermon or something.

And then, from out of the blue, a better-looking and younger reverend happens to arrive in town and shows an interest in her.

Fucking Laura seems to be the best way to take my first act of *settling old scores* where Leeson is involved. And he definitely doesn't have to know about it. I mean, I'd feel pretty bad if Maria found out and lost her notion of being part of such a happy family. Then there would be the risk of bumping into her years down the line and not recognising her whereas she would recognise me alright.

I smile as if at this little snapshot of family bliss, reach a hand into my pocket for my cigarettes. "Are you allowed to smoke in here?" I ask.

"I'm afraid not," Laura says, pulling a face to try and have me think she feels my pain. "But if you tell us what you're thinking of ordering," she adds, "you could go outside for a cigarette and we'll order it for you?"

"Betty is working out back today," Leeson happily says, dropping into the chair beside me and handing out the laminated menus he's brought over. "Betty's waffles are the best," he says for my benefit.

"Yeah?" I ask him with a smile of my own, "Are they just like momma used to make?"

"Sure," Leeson says with a smirk, clearly a little confused. He opens his menu and takes to examining it, probably trying to figure out just how exactly he came to be sitting next to such an oddball this morning.

"Hey," Maria says to me, "you won't believe who we saw in here one time last summer."

I politely ask her, "Who?"

"Guess," she insists.

"I don't know," I say, "Kyle Maclachlan?"

Maria laughs and asks, "Who's that?"

"I guess you're too young to know any of his better work," I smile. "But this place just reminds me so much of Lumberton," and I say to Leeson, "how about you? It's like Lumberton has spilled off the big screen, isn't it?" Before he can answer I turn my attention back to Maria and ask her, "Did I only have the one guess?"

"No," Maria giggles. "You can have one more and I mean that," she says, "just the one."

"Just the one," I say, drumming my fingers across the table. "Just the one… Was it Paul McCartney?" Maria laughs at that one. "Come on," I say, "you have to know who Paul McCartney is! Man made the bass guitar a real instrument. Man wrote some great songs and had a real good voice when he was younger."

"It's not that," Laura says from behind her own laughter, "she knows who Paul McCartney is. She just thinks it's hysterical when somebody mentions The Beatles because every once in a while, when she's trying to listen to some music in her room, *somebody*," she says while playfully pointing in Leeson's direction, "will play The Beatles at full volume if he thinks her music is a little too loud. He'll drown her out completely!"

"Well," I say to Leeson, "I think most people had a parent who thought The Beatles were just the best. Who's your favourite?" I ask him.

"Beatle? Paul," he says. "How about you?"

"Ringo," I lie. "But anyway," I say to Maria, "the suspense is killing me already. Who did you see here one summer?"

"George W. Bush," she says and I start laughing at her answer, remembering how Tiffany Lily had made out she knew him well all those years ago and I try to picture her sitting down in a place like this for something to eat. I laugh because almost every name I hear feels like it is somehow connected to someone I knew during another part of my life.

"I'm sorry," I say, still laughing, "I just remembered an old Jay Leno gag. But wow, George W. was in this place, huh? The waffles really must be good."

12

MARIA HAS A glass of Coke, the waitress being considerate enough to add ice *and* a slice of lemon to the drink without being asked, and us grown-ups each have a coffee; Laura having hers with cream whereas Leeson and I opt for plain black. The waffles are pretty good, too. They're not too dry and Maria has blueberries mixed into hers, which makes me a little jealous.

"So," Laura asks me, "where did you say you're from?"

"I didn't," I tell her and then I smile before continuing. "Originally," I say, "a small town. One of those places you'll be in for life if you don't get out of there during your late teens - not that I'm trying to encourage you here, sweetheart," I say to Maria with a warm smile. "I haven't been back there once since I left," I inform Laura, "and that was over ten years ago now."

"Ten years." She asks, "Don't you have any family back there?"

"Not really," I say, shaking my head. "My older brother left way before I did and I have no idea where he could be right now. We could have even been at the same restaurant once or twice during my travels and not known," I say with a smile and Laura smiles right back at me but it's one filled by sadness. "But I eventually settled down in Los Angeles after a little while," I tell her, "and was soon doing my bit to spread the good word."

"Los Angeles," Laura says, "wow. I'd love to go there, I really would."

"I'm pretty desperate to get out of there."

Laura asks, "Bad experience?"

"Too many of the churches I've dealt with over in Los Angeles are under the control of people who don't really give a damn - if you'll pardon my French."

"It's okay," she assures me with another smile before finally asking, "but what is the name of your church?"

"Saint Claire's," I tell her and I'm pretty sure Leeson goes real tense for a second on hearing that. I wish I could have been looking right at him when I'd said it but I didn't want to risk giving anything away. I think I'd only ever want him to find out for sure just who I am exactly once I had taken *everything* from him and sitting next to him right now, I'm undecided to how much I want to punish him for his past sins; the original sin being how he took off and left me.

"It was a nice place for a while," I add, "just don't ask me where they got the name from!"

Laura laughs and looks to Leeson, who merely smirks and goes on eating his waffles. His eyes are glued to the plate but I've a feeling he's listening to my every word like he would those of a newly returned Christ.

"These waffles," I declare, "really are special."

"Better than the kind they have in Los Angeles?" Maria asks me.

"Oh," I lie, "LA doesn't have any little places like this. It's nothing but big companies like McDonald's or Starbucks."

Leeson - without taking his eyes from his plate- asks me, "Who have you left watching over Saint Claire's during your vacation?"

"Just another reverend," I tell him. "Guy named Reverend Howard. He's real swell," I claim, "probably the second nicest man out there. The first being me, obviously."

"And you're travelling north," Leeson asks, "to visit family?"

"No," I say with a shake of my head, wondering if he's already suspecting me and trying to catch me out sooner rather than later, "it's a vacation but it's also a little more than that, if you understand? Somebody who used to attend Saint Claire's is having… well, having a crisis of sorts and I promised I'd go visit them once their own vacation starts."

Laura says in amazement, "You're really travelling all this way just to see them?"

"Beats talking with them over the telephone," I say with a smile. "Just because they don't attend my sermons these days, it doesn't mean I'll happily wash my hands of them. I don't think it's right," I say, pushing my now empty plate into the centre of the table, "to abandon somebody when they really need you."

"That's very noble," Laura tells me.

"If you don't like it out in Los Angeles," Maria asks, "can't you ask them to send you someplace else?"

"You've got me," I grin. "You're a very sharp kid, do you know that? I bet my mother was just like you when she was growing up. Another reason for my heading up north," I claim, "is I've been told there's a church there soon to be in need of a new reverend. What can I say?" I smirk, "If the locals already know me and like me, it's more than likely I'll be given the gig. The four of us eating together like this could become a regular thing if I'm not too far away."

Leeson finishes his waffles and looks to me with a quizzical expression. "You're not sure how far away the place you're headed to is from here?"

"I can't drive," I say with a shrug. "Most parents are happy to teach their kids how to drive, but mine…" I pause, hoping Leeson is hanging on to hear if I'm about to mention an old Ford left to rust in front of the family home, "couldn't drive," I finish. "How funny is that," I ask them, "in this day and age? My old man didn't even own an automatic!"

Maria says, "What about your mom?"

"I don't know," I say like it's a real pain for me to do so. "She wasn't really in my life all that much."

13

I find the Four Card motel on Central Street without too much difficulty but the look of the place surprises me. It's like a fallen rectangle of concrete with six plain doors and six windows evenly spread out along it. I'd at least been expecting two storeys and an outdoor pool that you wouldn't take a dip in but you can leave your bottles of beer in there until they cool down enough. Noticing how the doors are simply numbered one through to six, I wonder what it is exactly I'm meant to do with there being no clear office to call at. I look for a sign holding a number to call and on failing that I simply try to look in through the windows but the net curtains behind them make it all but impossible.

I'm still trying to look inside window number three when a man, Mitch, I'm assuming, comes marching out of door number one. He's short and real fat with grey curly hair. I turn to face him and he drops the aggressive stance he was modelling, like that is the best way to attract business. The top three, four buttons of his shirt are unbuttoned and you can see a chest of damp hair because of it. "Hey," he says to me, "can I help you?" His eyes keep moving from mine to the collar I'm wearing.

"Hi," I say with a grin, taking my first steps toward him. "I'm Reverend Doyle," I begin, "and Reverend Leeson told me to come here and find Mitch." I don't tell him how Leeson was more than a little off come the time I left him and his delightful family, like he was still trying to figure me out for a part of him was already screaming out: *Don't trust this guy!* I know if Mitch says he hasn't a room for me, it'll mean Leeson managed to sneak away from his wife and daughter to make a call to him.

"Oh," the man smiles, "I'm Mitch," and right away I know Leeson didn't manage to make the call. "You say Leeson told you to come by here?" he asks, offering me his hand. Stubby fingers with a cheap ring on each one. I shake it anyway and find it to be damp with sweat. I want to wipe my hand against my jeans like Doyle did after I first saw him shaking Chambers' hand but manage not to.

"He sure did," I say. "I'm staying in town for a week or so," I continue, turning a little to let him catch a glimpse of my rucksack, "and he told me you were the man to see."

"Sure," Mitch blushes, "I can sort you a room, no problem. You have any preference?" he asks like the sight of an outside door or window is enough for me to see.

I joke, "How about one where I'm allowed to smoke?"

Mitch laughs. "You can smoke in any of the rooms," he says, "just leave the window open. But stay right here," he says heading back into the first room, "and I'll go and get you a key."

He disappears inside for a moment and comes back out carrying a key. "Let's see what's behind door number three," he jokes, solely because that was the door he found me at. He turns the key in the lock and pushes the door open. I follow him inside. The room is reasonably big but smells a little stale, like the window has been closed a long time. There's a mattress on a metal cot, a bedside dresser with lamp and a small TV- not to mention the obligatory framed painting of a lake on one of the walls. "Bathroom is right through there," he says pointing at the door to the right, "and there's a Bible in the drawer of the bedside table," he grins, "just in case you forgot your own."

"This will do me," I say. "How much is it for-"

"Darn," he interrupts me on looking to the TV. "Hold on for one sec', would you?"

He unplugs the TV from the wall, lifts it in his flabby arms and walks out with it. Apart from where the TV was recently placed, the stand it was on is over an inch thick with dust. A little confused, I shake my head and take a look at the bathroom. It's like somebody has tiled the inside of a wardrobe and fixed a washbasin beside a walk-in shower it's that small. You probably have to close the door behind you before you can sit down on the toilet, otherwise your knees will get in the way when you try to get a little privacy.

"Here we are," Mitch joyfully announces on returning to the

room with another TV to place on the stand. "That last one," he explains, "would have seen you dropping a quarter for every half hour of TV. This one," he says, "is just an ordinary TV. Rooms come with cable, too."

"That's very kind of you," I tell him. "But how much do the rooms cost?"

Mitch says, "You're here for a week?"

"Maybe a little longer."

"How about," he says, "how about… fifty dollars for six days and nights seeing as you're a reverend and a friend of Leeson? That's the best deal I can offer at the moment."

"That's very kind," I tell him, "and more than enough."

Mitch smiles proudly as he looks over his room, good deed in place. "So will you be helping out around the church while you're here?"

"Only if I'm needed," I say with a smile. "This is more of a brief vacation for me."

"Hey," Mitch asks with a smile, "who doesn't need one of those right now?"

"Tell me about it."

Mitch smiles again and goes back to looking over his room with pride. "Hey," he says as the question hits him, "did Leeson warn you about Sam?"

I ask, "Sam?"

Mitch chuckles, claps his hands with glee. "You didn't hear this from me," he says, "but watch out around Sam Pennington."

"Okay," I say with a smile and a nod, "but who is he?"

"*She*," he gladly corrects me. "Lone parent with a son who's going through a rebellious phase. She was trying to have Leeson guide him some, but that's not all she was after."

"Oh?"

"You know," Mitch says and he runs a tongue over his sticky lips, "what they say about a man in uniform…? Well, I'm sure you'll have heard similar stories during your time."

"Yeah," I tell him, "I get you."

"Leeson feels real guilty because he tries to avoid her these days, but she was trying to seduce him! He told me all about it - in confidence, of course."

"Of course."

"She tends to go for drinks in *Velma's* so if you go there to wet your whistle, beware the woman talking about an unruly son needing guidance!"

"I will," I laugh.

"Okay," he says, "I'll go get you some clean towels before I leave you to settle in and if you need anything at all, you can usually find me over in number one."

"Thanks." I ask him, "So should I pay you now?"

"No," he says, waving his hands as he slowly backs out of the door. "We'll settle it when you're ready to make tracks."

14

STANDING IN THE open doorway of my motel room, I watch the passing cars while smoking a cigarette. And I spend a lot of time thinking.

I just can't forget how Mitch came and knocked on the door only a couple of minutes after he had left me with the rough but clean towels he had just brought over. He had a real sorry look on his face and he was keeping his eyes down as he spoke. A part of me had thought he had come back just to say he had looked over the books and it turned out he couldn't let me have the room for so cheap after all. But it wasn't that. Mitch had wanted to apologise.

"I'm sorry," he'd said, "if I caused any offense, what with laughing at how Sam is in lust with Leeson. I wasn't trying to… cheapen your profession," he'd said. "I guess it isn't so funny, having some women wanting to bed you as a challenge, or to prove something to themselves, maybe… Men like you and Leeson do nothing but try and help us all out, and you're an inspiration for it. You all deserve more than to be gossiped about around town," he'd said, "or thought less of because of how some others go and act around you."

I'd told him I'd taken no offence and that it was real good of him to come by anyway.

But now, I just can't shake off the idea he gave me, just like I can't lose my grin.

Screwing Laura Leeson is still the ultimate goal for me. Screw her and leave this home of hers not long after. Leave him wondering why his old lady is acting so funny all of a sudden, like she's trying to hide something or she's feeling a little guilty. You know, that could even *save* their marriage, the guilt making her become a little distant which, in return, would have the clearly sexually impotent husband start trying a lot harder around her. No pun intended.

But with Sam Pennington, I could do some real damage. I could do some irreparable damage. My logic is simple; that I also fuck her and leave town not long after. Mitch's warning has left me with no doubt whatsoever that she'd soon be dropping hints here and there to what we got up to. She won't openly admit it, but she'll plant the seeds amongst the locals. And with me not being here to stamp my foot down on any developing stems, they'll continue to grow and soon everybody in town will be talking about how Sam Pennington screwed a travelling reverend. A reverend that had to leave soon after because of his terrible guilt.

A reverend that Leeson himself must be good friends with, because people had seen them dining together and Leeson helped him get a room for a good price over at the Four Card…

I won't settle for tainting his family life, oh no. I'll taint his career and how people look at him. I'll leave a stain upon him brighter than any scarlet letter could be. And I smile, wondering just how Laura will react once she hears she wasn't the only conquest of mine.

Still smiling, I flick my cigarette into the road and step back into my room, closing the door behind me. Mitch had mentioned a bar, a place called Velma's, and that is where I'll be going in search of Sam Pennington and her carnal desires. But first it'd probably be a good idea for me to take a shower.

Entering the bathroom, I grin turning on the light. The illuminated bulb would been used to represent my latest idea if life were a cartoon. I've decided that when the time comes to leave town, I'm going to creep out early one morning without settling my bill with Mitch. Doing so will hopefully taint the friendship between him and the good reverend. Doing all of the above will see my brother become more than an outcast… It will be his turn to feel abandoned.

15

Velma's is pretty quiet, especially given that it's already after eight o'clock. I wonder if it's just that people have to be up early for work tomorrow or maybe it's just not the most favoured bar out in Whicker. There are hardly any women drinking here, just men with stubble or bushy moustaches, and I wonder what I'll do if I don't get to meet Sam Pennington. I doubt I can afford to come back here night after night. Actually, I know I can't, but I make my way to the bar regardless. A couple of guys playing pool glance up at me as I pass, the one about to take a shot probably hoping I'm a good omen for him due to the collar around my throat. Wondering just why it is Leeson doesn't wear one I reach for my cigarettes but stop myself, remembering how maybe you're not allowed to here - and a bar of all places! America isn't really sure who she is anymore.

I take my place at the bar and wait to be served. There are one or two other guys already standing there, already intoxicated enough to be making a little too much noise, and a lone guy propped up on a stool with a glass of dark liquid to hand - Guinness, I assume - as he picks at the dry roasted peanuts in a bowl out in front of him. He's dressed a little scruffily, has a beard that could do with trimming and a lot of gel in his black hair that makes it look like he doesn't wash it. Despite this, he's pretty handsome for a guy. That's probably what makes him sure enough of himself to smirk on noticing my dog collar, but he doesn't say anything about it.

"What can I get you?" a youngish barman asks me.

"I don't suppose you sell Whicker's Best," I joke. That's the thing with me; always cracking funnies nobody else will get.

"No," he says shaking his head, "I haven't even heard of it."

"Just a Heineken," I say. He nods, pours my drink and hands it over. I pay him and leave a small tip. Let him think the travelling preacher has little enough money as it is - which is true in this case.

"What are you," the guy behind the peanut bowl asks me, "a reverend, a father- what?" His accent isn't American. In fact, it's a little hard for me to place. Impossible, even.

"Reverend," I tell him. "My name's Reverend Doyle," I say with hopes of my name already being known long before I leave, "and I'm just passing through here."

"Same here," the guy with the peanuts says.

The barman stops wiping down the bar just long enough to ask me, "You know Reverend Leeson?"

"Sure," I smile, "he's a great man." I say that so it'll sound like I knew him real well when it's time for me to leave *but* if Leeson is asked about me before that day comes, it won't make him suspicious... Won't sound too much like I'm making out I know him well for a reason he can't yet understand.

"He's okay," the barman says with a nod, then adding like it's no big deal to mention, "he got my cousin Mitch over his coke problem." My heart lights up on hearing that. It's only a little information but it reveals a hell of a lot about their friendship, why Mitch clearly thinks he owes him something. And it's something I could use to my advantage if I just had the time to think of how.

The barman turns and walks away, off to do whatever else he has to do. I hear somebody laugh real loud so I turn to see what it is. A middle aged woman is laughing as the guy she's with drunkenly drops coins into the side of the mechanical bull in the corner of the room, no doubt desperate to impress her by showing how long he can remain on it. Looking over at the woman in question I realise if she is Sam Pennington, she's already found the guy she's taking back home tonight and so my trip here is nothing if not a waste of my time and money. The guy with the peanuts eventually says to make conversation, "I considered being a reverend once."

"Oh yeah?" I ask him, "What happened?"

"Nothing," he says. "I wanted to be a reverend because I thought it would be one day's work a week for good money and a home the church is willing to pay for, but then a friend told me I'd have to be visiting people dying in a hospital bed and shit like that. That's what put me off," he shrugs. "I just wanted an easy job… I can't say I'm a big believer in God or anything like that."

"Me neither," I say like I'm joking and the guy laughs. "What is that you're drinking, anyway?" I ask him.

"This?" He tilts his glass to get a better look inside of it like he's already forgotten what it is he ordered. "Guinness and blackcurrant," he says. "Best way to drink Guinness," he adds.

"Right," I laugh. "A whole lot of Irishmen want a word with you out-back."

"I hope not."

I chuckle and we're silent for a little while. Eventually I say, "Your accent is a little unusual for around here. Where are you from?"

"Originally? Liverpool," he says.

"As in England?"

"That's the place," he nods.

"You're far from home," I say. That would make two of us.

"I don't have one," he says. "I'm just moving along until I find somewhere to stay. Wherever it is, it isn't in England."

"What makes you say that?" I ask him out of interest.

"I'm a republican," he says, "in the sense I don't want or believe in a royal family. The term sort of has a different meaning over here."

"I guess it does."

"But a few years back," he continues, "Prince William and his piece had their kid and the news reports went on about it like we were all excited for them, but I wasn't. Nobody I knew was excited for them. It actually made us wish we were French," he adds and it makes me laugh. "But then I wondered what it would be like, if I had kids of my own and then, years down the line, the new heir or eventual spare had kids and the news reports got all excited about it again. Can you imagine," he asks, "my kids turning to me and asking *why* I didn't do anything to get rid of the royal family when I was younger? Why did I allow them to stay in place?

"And I'd have to say I always hoped somebody else would take care of the revolution for me," he sighs. "So I left as soon as I came into a little money thanks to my writing." He grins, adding, "I don't want to risk having children in a country where others can be born into power; I don't believe in that at all. I'll go back to England once the royals are gone," he says bringing his drink to his lips, "but I don't think that's ever going to happen. Not in my lifetime, anyway."

"It's good to have principles," I offer. "What's your name, anyway?"

"Alec," he says. "What's yours again?"

"Reverend Doyle," I tell him, "it's a pleasure to meet you."

"And you," he nods as we shake hands.

"Listen," I ask him, "could you watch my drink while I just head to the bathroom?"

"Sure," he says with a nod, "go right ahead."

I make my way to the bathroom, taking a good look at the woman laughing as her potential suitor struggles to stay atop of a mechanical bull. She glances over at me but then goes back to looking at the other guy so I figure she isn't Sam Pennington anyway. In the bathroom, a coat is hanging over the locked door of a cubical. The pocket on display is fat, suggesting a wallet is inside, so I quietly kneel down and take a peek under the door. Polished shoes and dropped pants look right back at me. I straighten up and carefully reach inside the coat pocket. Just as I had expected, the wallet is nestled within. Faux leather with two twenties and a ten inside. Seriously, making it so easy for somebody to lift fifty dollars from him, the guy's lucky I'm too nice to swipe it all. I only pocket one of the available twenties, telling myself it will teach the man not to be so trusting in this kind of place, and then I take a leak before washing my hands and returning to the bar.

Alec finishes what's left of his drink and stands. "I've got to go," he explains, "I'm getting the next train out of here."

"Isn't it a little late?"

"Nah," he says, "I've already ordered a room at a hotel a couple of miles from here. But you enjoy your time in Whicker."

"I will," I assure him. "Good luck finding someplace to call home."

"Thanks," he laughs, extracting a cigarette from the pack he takes from his pocket. I wait for him to light up where he's standing before asking if you can smoke here. "Sure can," he says, "but I'm finding it confusing out in America; hard to tell what's law and what's not when it comes to smoking in a lot of places."

"Here, here," I tell him. "Spare a man of God a smoke?"

"Sure," he says passing me one. "You take care of yourself."

16

I WAKE UP because the bed is shaking. At first I wonder if this is one of those beds some places have, where you drop in a dollar or something and it vibrates for a little while, but then I gather enough of my senses to realise I didn't slip a dollar into it and it sounds like a train is going by on the street outside. Feeling more than a little curious I get out of the bed and head over to the window, moving the curtain aside to get a look. A large truck with Rhea Lumber along its side is disappearing further down the road and you can feel the windowsill vibrating due to the weight of the moving vehicle. I yawn, move away from the window and look to the bed. I know I won't manage to fall back to sleep now and it's only a little after five o'clock.

"Fuck it," I mutter and I stand at the open doorway in only my underwear so I can enjoy the first cigarette of the morning. The breeze is a pleasant temperature. Seagulls are hanging out overhead, screeching like crazy for whatever reason, and I wonder how their screaming hadn't woken me a little earlier. A white van that should have been cleaned a week ago at least comes to a stop outside the motel. A man in overalls steps out of the vehicle holding a collection of newspapers kept together with knotted string and tosses them at door number one before returning to his vehicle and driving on.

My eyes keep darting back and forth, surveying the empty street before settling back down on the bundle of newspapers. I consider rushing over to them, taking one or two before rushing back here, but decide against it. Unless Mitch orders some respectable newspapers (I have no idea why he's having so many delivered, unless you get a complimentary paper for every day you're a guest at the motel), I doubt there'll be anything worth reading anyway. News about little assholes like Justin Bieber, and not the news you're waiting for where he's involved e.g. the prick has finally gone and died, or directors making new movies with little heart but plenty of special effects and computer generated explosions and that's mostly it. They feed us this shit so we overlook the smaller articles. Articles about unmanned drones wiping out entire families over in the Middle East. Articles about corrupt politicians. Articles about men who are stupid enough to try and make an honest living so they can look after their family who are now losing more of their rights.

But who gives a fuck about any of that? Let's all read about the latest teen-sensation. Not that I hold any resentment to those who would, you know, rather see stories about nonentities than acts of atrocity. It's just that I'd rather turn a blind eye to them than pretend they're not really happening. Trust me, there's a difference between the two.

17

THERE'S NO MESSAGE spelled out on the board outside the church and I wonder if it could be Leeson hasn't arrived yet. It's still that awkward hour of day, when some people are already walking into their place of work whereas others are only just making their way there. Standing outside, I notice a couple of rubberneckers going by in their cars and how they look at me, trying to figure out just who I am exactly and what I'm doing outside Leeson's place of business. That's what makes me flick my cigarette away before I've smoked a full half of it and make my way toward the entrance. The doors are unlocked, one of them standing wide open to permit entry. My footsteps echo because of the stone floor, so I move along as quietly as I can. For a while I don't see anybody and I figure the place is empty, but then I take a gander behind a door left standing ajar and see Leeson. He's got his back to me and he's on his knees, silently praying before a statue of Jesus on the cross. And it takes all of my control not to laugh. I mean, does he really believe a glorified plastic ornament made in Taiwan is going to act as his own hotline to Heaven?

But I know what I need to know, that he's already here, so I creep back outside and pace around the grounds of the church with a perplexed expression on my face. I let a couple of people pass me by without moving in their direction, like I don't even notice the way they're looking at me, but then I spot a sweet-looking old lady and rush over to her. "Excuse me," I say, trying my best to sound like I'm a little ashamed at how I'm bothering her like this.

"Can I help you?" she asks, trying her best to be pleasant. The gold cross she's wearing around her neck probably means she *has* to offer assistance to those in need.

"This is real embarrassing," I say, "but I urgently need to talk with Paul - I mean Reverend Leeson," I add as if to correct

66

myself, "but I'm having some trouble finding him."

The old lady momentarily stands on her tiptoes, looking over my shoulder and towards the church before lowering herself back down to look me in the eye. "He's not inside the church?" she asks.

"It doesn't look like it," I sigh. "I've got his home address written down, but it's just that I left it in my room at the Four Card motel." I sigh again, shake my head before continuing. "I don't want to walk all the way back there to get his address, then head over to his place and find he's gone someplace else before I can have a word with him."

The old woman looks me over for a minute. "I saw you yesterday," she says, eyes squinted as she continues to examine my face, "didn't I?"

"Maybe," I tell her. "I was standing just here with Laura and Maria for a little while, then we all went out for waffles together."

"That's Reverend Leeson for you," she laughs, "it was a nice day yesterday…"

"Tell me about it," I say, "he'd walk everywhere if it was down to him - rain or shine."

The woman nods as if in understanding. "And it is important that you talk with him?" she asks.

"Very," I tell her. "Like you would not believe!"

"Okay," she says with a nod, and then she gives me his home address.

"You're an angel," I tell her. "But could you help me out with how to get there exactly? I'm still learning my way around this quaint little town of yours."

Leeson and his family reside in a nice little two-storey home in a street that is just as nice. Only a few people have picket fences to keep others from their well-maintained lawns, the rest just spill out onto the street and yet there isn't a single dog turd to be seen on any of them. And I approach his whitewashed home with confident steps and a bouquet of flowers in my arms. Before I press the doorbell, I spot the sign beside the door - it looks like a thin chunk has been taken from a log - varnished and then had GOD BLESS THIS HOUSE engraved onto it. I press the doorbell, take a single step back and wait.

"Oh," Laura says, smiling with surprise on seeing me as she opens the door to see who it is. She must have been tidying up or something because she's wearing a sunflower yellow pair of those rubber gloves some people wear for washing the dishes. "Reverend Doyle," she politely asks, "what are you doing here?" Seeing those rubber gloves on her hands, I can't help but wish she had gone straight out and asked what she could *do* for me. A hand-job with those things on would be a whole new experience.

"Thanking my favourite family for helping me find a place to stay," I answer on holding up the flowers for her to take. The way her eyes light up tells me it's been a long time since her husband was thoughtful enough to go out and buy her some flowers. If I had any doubts at all that he's been ignoring her, they all fall away on seeing how much she likes them.

"You really shouldn't have," she blushes, accepting the bouquet. "They must have cost a lot of money."

"Actually," I say like I'm only kidding, "I swiped them from outside the flower store because the owner was a little preoccupied."

"Well," she laughs, "I know reverends aren't the best paid people in the world! I don't know what to say," she says, "thank you."

"It was no big deal."

"But it's a wonderful gesture. I'm sorry," she says like she genuinely is, "but Paul isn't here."

"He isn't?"

"I'm afraid not," she says, "he's already over at the church."

"Oh," I chuckle, "well, okay. I'll start walking over there," I say, slowly turning around, "but it was a pleasure to see you again."

"Wait," she says, and I stop and slowly turn back around like I have no idea to what she could be about to say. "Would you like to come in for a cup of coffee?" she asks. "It'll give you a chance to rest your feet for a while before you have to start walking again."

"I really don't want to be a bother," I say, taking a discreet step closer to the front door.

"Don't be silly," she assures me, "come right on in."

"Thank you," I smile, accepting her offer.

"We don't have many people visit us here," Laura says, leading us towards the living room which in turn will lead us into the kitchen. "Everybody tends to go straight over to the church," she adds, and I can't escape the feeling that she's telling me this as if to explain why, in her eyes, the house is a little untidy when it really isn't.

"I was going to head over to the church," I joke, "but thought people could get the wrong idea if they saw me giving Paul those flowers."

Laura laughs at the gag and just as we're walking through the living room I hear Tiffany Lily say from behind me, "Well, I was wondering when exactly you'd turn up here."

18

My heart freezes. I quickly turn on my heels to see Tiffany, or what Tiffany has become. Tiffany is almost unrecognisable now; she looks to have had cheek implants, her face is too tight and practically expressionless, her lips all the more swollen. Even her eyes have lost their natural spark and are now glassy, glazed over. She could be the poster girl for the extraterrestrial beings Scientologists worship. Well, extraterrestrial beings with a lot of money.

"Well," she says from behind the TV screen - eyes staring someplace off camera; lips moving slightly while her jaw remains still, "isn't this exactly what you were expecting to happen?"

She's replaced by a shot of a youngish man standing in a kitchen, shaking his head as if in disbelief as he drops sliced fruit into a blender. Despite the false alarm and my knowledge that Tiffany can't see or hear me, that the scene I have just witnessed could have been shot *months* ago, my heart seems to be having a little difficulty in slowing back down.

"You watch this, too?" Laura asks, sounding a little guilty. "I just had to start watching it again this week," she smirks, "because they're about to reveal who put Chester in a coma."

"Wow," I say, turning to face her like I'm feeling okay, turning to face her like I have any idea to what she is talking about. "Who do you think did it?" I ask her.

"Maybe Jessica," she says, "maybe Bobby. But what do you think," she asks with a smile, "should we have our coffees out in the kitchen or do you want to have them in here?"

Tiffany, or what was once Tiffany, comes back on screen and struggles to display emotion. It's seeing her again that has me turn to Laura and say as calmly as I can, "Do you mind if we still head into the kitchen? I'll catch this on rerun and I'd like to avoid spoilers…"

"Ha," Laura says, turning to head back for the kitchen, "that's what I was hoping you'd say." I take one last look at the TV screen before following her. I take one last look at Tiffany and wonder if the surgery was anything to do with something Chambers had suggested. I wonder if Cole is still with her and what he thinks of her new appearance, if the two of them are sharing their bed with a third person once again. They could even be sharing their bed with a woman this time, because I hear the whole bisexual scene is back in fashion out in Hollywood.

And then I turn and calmly walk into the kitchen. The layout reminds me of the kitchen back at home but a lot more light is spilling in through the windows. A part of me wonders if Leeson has arranged the kitchen like this so he will have a feeling of doing *something* right if a child in such surroundings becomes a happy, well-adjusted adult. I'd have never have set my kitchen out like this... Even the sunlight has me thinking back to my own early years; trying to determine whether the days were always grey and cold like I remember them being or if I insist on remembering them being like that.

"Take a seat," Laura joyfully says to me, pouring coffee into a couple of white cups. I sit at *my* side of the table. The scar on my hand starts to itch but I only glance at it for the most fleeting of moments. She asks me, "Do you take sugar and cream?"

"Sugar," I say, "please."

"How many?"

Without meaning to I say, "Five."

"Five," she laughs, "are you serious?"

"I'm serious," I tell her with a smirk. "Five sugars."

"Ha," she says, "I'm wondering if I should even inquire how *that* habit came about."

"My dad," I lie. Still smiling, I reach a hand into my pocket and ask her, "Do you mind if I have a cigarette?"

"No problem," she says, taking a clean ashtray from a nearby cupboard, placing it down on the table. "It'll be nice to have a cup of coffee and a cigarette with somebody else for a change."

I tell her, "I thought you said you don't smoke."

"Just don't tell Paul," she smiles, bringing our drinks over to the table and placing them down before sitting opposite me. "I'll have to drop the cigarette ends down the gutter, clean the ashtray and air the house out before he returns home," she smiles mischievously. "I never told him I took up smoking again a year or two after Maria was born. I didn't admit to that yesterday," she says, "because I thought the two of you might have known one or two of the same people."

I take a cigarette for myself out of the pack and then a second for her, feeling like I'm already getting one over Leeson as I hand it over. "Does Maria know you smoke?"

"Maria knows I'll have a cigarette from time to time," she nods, accepting the cigarette. "I think she likes the idea of us having a secret only we know about," she adds and it makes me feel happy, like I'm using them both in a way. I light my cigarette before sliding the Zippo over to her.

"Interesting inscription," she says, lighting her own.

"It was my old man's light," I explain.

"So how did your dad get you taking five sugars in your coffee?" she immediately asks, smiling as she hands the lighter back to me.

I answer, "Just a story he used to enjoy telling when I was young," smirking as I shake my head like I find the whole thing to be silly but I've told it a million times before regardless. "He was on an army exercise," I continue, "and they could only carry a limited amount of stock, so everybody in the group decides to leave their sugar behind, as you would," I offer in explanation, "because you can handle unsweetened drinks for a while if you have to, right?"

"Right," Laura answers with a smile.

"Wrong," I chuckle, pausing to drag a little smoke into my lungs just to keep her hanging. "Everybody in the group ends up real cranky and tired, and it's all because they ditched the sugar. That was the point of the exercise, you see? Sometimes you really will need what you figure you can do without. So dad took to telling me that story *all* of the time at one stage or another during my early years," I sigh, "and it made me the man who can only drink coffee if it's holding five sugars."

Laura laughs. "I'm amazed you've still got all of your own teeth," she says.

"So am I."

"But your dad," she eventually asks just to keep the conversation rolling, "was he a general or a lieutenant… anything like that?"

"Nah," I say, shaking my head. "He was working in a mill come the time I was old enough to know what was going on around me. Acting as a preacher not long after that," I add, wondering how long it will take for the information to reach Leeson and what he will make of it on hearing it.

Laura laughs again. "I'm sorry," she says, "but going from the army to the church? God, I don't even know why I even find that so funny."

"It kind of is," I say, "especially if he really was in the army."

Laura seems to perk up, hearing that. "What do you mean?" she asks from behind a curious smile.

"Well," I shrug, "I never saw a single picture of dad in his army uniform. Never found it in a chest up in the attic. Sometimes," I tell her, "I just wonder if he went and made the whole thing up."

"To impress you," she asks, "when you were a boy?"

"Maybe," I say. "But think about it, I just told you a story from my childhood, right? But what if it was all a lie I told - just for the hell of it? You know what my old roommate out in LA used to say? He said if just a part of you believes in the lie you're giving, everybody else will believe every word of it."

"It wasn't," she smiles, looking more than a little proud.

I want to know, "What makes you so sure?" and Laura runs a finger along her neck in response. After a moment or two I laugh, realising how she's pointing out the collar I'm wearing. "Okay," I grin, "so using myself for this was a bad example. But just think about it," I explain, "when you meet somebody for the first time… You really can tell them *anything* you want. You can tell them the truth or a variation of it, and they'll just have to take your word for it, just like my believing you were a non-smoker. But you can make yourself sound as smart or as funny or as interesting as you want to, can't you? Even claim a good friend's experience as one of your own.

And now think of parents," I chuckle. "We never really know who they are, but we believe everything they tell us is true. They spend years lying to us about Santa Claus and when we're old enough they tell us he doesn't exist. We go from believing in him to knowing he was never there in the blink of an eye, and it's all down to the trust in our parents."

"But that's exactly my point," Laura says, "about your father maybe lying about being in the army just to impress you a little? Sure, our parents lied about Santa Claus, but wasn't that just to make the holidays that little bit special for us?"

"No," I smirk, "they lied so we'd act the way they wanted us to, if only for a while."

She laughs again. "So why lie to me?" She asks, "How is it you want me to act?"

"You've already called me out," I smirk, "you know I'm not lying. I'll never know for sure if dad was or wasn't speaking the truth about being in the army, but sometimes I just like to wonder how much we really know about the people we encounter. In a way," I sigh, "we try and have the people around us viewing us the way we wish we were. We hope we'll appear as confident as we want to be. As funny… as intellectual."

"As slim," she jokes.

"As slim," I laugh. "Five sugars in every cup of coffee means you have to exercise more than most people, anyway." Laura laughs again and we're quiet for a little while. Eventually I say to her, "Can I just ask you something, about what we were saying about how people view us?"

"Sure," she says.

"I notice Paul doesn't wear a collar. Why is that?"

"Everybody in town knows he's the reverend," she says like it's that simple. "He'll wear it from time to time, on special occasions, but not all of the time. It's just that he doesn't really need to."

"Did he used to," I ask her, "when he first arrived in town?"

"Sure," Laura says with a nod. "Before people got to know him."

"But do you really know him," I grin, "or do you just see him the way he wants you to?”

19

LAURA JOINS ME in a second cigarette and I imagine Leeson returning home and detecting it, just a little, despite how hard she tries to rid the room of the smell. And I imagine Leeson picturing me and remembering how I'm a smoker as he looks back at the flowers I brought and he can't help but wonder how long I was here and what me and the wife talked about…

I drink a little coffee and stub my cigarette out in the ashtray before asking Laura, "Would it be okay for me to use your bathroom?"

"Sure," she nods, "it's just right at the top of the stairs."

"Thanks," I say with a smile and I leave the kitchen, make my way up the stairs and find the bathroom with the door already standing open. I close it over, just so it'll look like I'm in there, before looking down the open landing.

There's a door on the wall to my left, standing right beside the stairs, and I push it open and slowly take my first step inside the room. I'd assumed it would be Laura and Leeson's room but it clearly isn't; the clothes littered across the floor and the posters on the wall let me know that it's Maria's room I'm in. She has posters of Katy Perry up on the wall and her rack looks so good in them. She'd be the perfect woman if it wasn't for the shit records or 'quirky' persona. Frozen and silent, she can never offend.

And then there are the pictures of one of the boys from One Direction, and they're not even pictures of the one who's supposed to be a real swordsman or the one with the coiffure haircut who always looks to be snarling. They're pictures of the blond guy; the one you look at and think he must have been half a gene away or something from being born a full retard.

Every picture she has of him, he looks back with those glassy eyes and jaw that's almost hanging wide open.

I hear a sharp intake of breath come from behind me and I

turn, expecting to find Laura has come up here to put a little washing away and found me exploring her teenage daughter's bedroom. But it isn't Laura, it's Maria. Maria holding a soft towel around her to cover her modesty, beads of water on her exposed skin shining like jewels. Even the towel she's wrapped around her hair reminds me of a turban, making her the Eastern princess. "I'm sorry," she says, "I didn't know you were in here."

"No," I tell her, "I'm sorry. I was looking for the bathroom and I took a wrong turn."

"Oh," she says.

"So this is your room?"

"Yes," she says. "I keep meaning to redecorate but can't find the time."

"Where does it all go? But why aren't you in school today?" I ask her.

"Free period."

"Oh," I chuckle, "of course. I didn't know if people were still using that."

"Using *what*?" she smiles.

"Free period," I reply. "I used to say I had a free period a couple of times a year, just to get a break from school. Whose handwriting have you mastered?" She smiles but it looks like she doesn't want to answer that one so I start talking again. "Let me guess," I say, "let me guess... Is it your mom's? I could imagine you two already having similar handwriting, so you just have to add an extra loop to a letter here and there and that's it. Am I right?"

"You're right," she blushes.

"I knew I would be. So what's your excuse for missing class today?"

"Dental appointment."

"Yeah," I nod, "I had a lot of those. The trick is to take time off here and there with apparent throat infections. That way, you can claim to have two dental appointments pretty close together," I advise her, "because you can say the dentist couldn't take a proper look at you last time, what with your throat or tonsils being inflamed."

Maria chuckles. "And you grew up to become a reverend," she says.

"Believe it or not," I tell her, "you don't require much of an education to do it. You certainly don't have to be truthful," I decide to add.

Maria laughs a little and I laugh alongside her. It's weird, how comfortable she seems despite me being in her room when she is only wearing a cotton towel. And looking at her also reminds me of my first thoughts toward her when we first met. She's a beautiful girl, maybe the most beautiful you could ever see. If Eleanor had looked like her, maybe I'd still be out in Sinclair. I want to light a cigarette but don't, just in case her mom suddenly calls up to make sure I'm okay.

"So you were just showering?" I ask her, feeling a little confused at how I didn't walk in on her in the bathroom.

"Yeah," she blushes again.

"I didn't see you in there. Not that I was hoping to see you in there," I quickly add.

"Mom and dad have an en-suite," she blushes like she can't stop herself now. "I prefer using that one. The amount of times I've walked out of the bathroom at the top of the stairs and a visitor has been standing at the front door..." she says with a smile and a shake of her head.

"Yeah," I nod. "But how about Katy Perry, eh?" I ask, drawing attention to her posters. "You like One Direction?"

"Not as much as I used to," she says, feeling a little embarrassed. Like only a little kid should listen to One Direction, and she would be wrong to think that. Only fucking retards should listen to One Direction. "I've outgrown them."

"Yeah," I say with a nod, "that'll be happening with a lot of things now. You're turning into a very beautiful woman." She blushes again and I smile at her. "Anyway," I say, walking back to the door, "your mom will be wondering where I am. But it was a real treat seeing you like this."

"Reverend Doyle?"

"Yeah?"

"You're staying at the Four Card, aren't you?"

"I sure am," I reply, nodding my head just the once. "Room number three."

"Room number three," she repeats back at me. "I have a friend who lives near there… Maybe I could come over and visit you some time… If you'd like?"

"That'd be real nice," I tell her, "you coming by when you get the chance… I'll try and make sure I have something nice to drink, just in case you do."

She smiles at me and says, voice trembling, "I'll be over sooner than you think."

20

LAURA IS REFILLING our coffees when I walk back into the kitchen and she has opened the backdoor as well as the windows to try and chase out the smell of cigarette smoke. "Somebody sure wants to keep her secret," I joke, returning to my chair.

"Is it that obvious?" she laughs.

"A little," I say, extracting a cigarette from the pack. "You having another?"

"No thank you," she replies. "Have you always been such a heavy smoker?"

"I don't know," I shrug while lighting up. "I always smoke what I can afford. But this place," I say, "I don't live in a place anywhere near as nice as this and I never have. Maybe if I wasn't smoking all my money away, I'd have a better place to rest my head."

"That's a lot like what Paul says. He doesn't smoke and he rarely drinks, so he always has a little money in his pocket."

"Smart man," I say, "but what about you? I mean, do you work or are you a lady of leisure?"

"Ha! I work," Laura says with a shrug, "but not full time. I'm a classroom assistant for children with learning difficulties every once in a while, and I give piano lessons two or three times a week. It's really just to get out of the house from time to time," she admits, letting me know for certain that she's the neglected housewife. The neglected housewife with a hot daughter coming into season, anyway…

"What about your family?" I ask her, "Do your parents still live in town?"

"No," she says, "they took retirement a couple of years back, bought a nice little place out in Florida. We usually stay with them for a while during the summer holidays."

"That's nice," I nod. "And what about Paul's family?" I ask her, "You ever see them or does he ever talk with them over the telephone?"

"No," she says, "we haven't even talked about his upbringing for years. He grew up in a care home," she tells me, "and he left to join the church as soon as he had the chance. Sometimes I wonder if he only joined the church to get out of there, sometimes I wonder if he just liked the idea of something loving him no matter what."

"No matter what," I softly repeat on bringing my coffee to my lips. "But it all worked out well for him in the end, didn't it?"

"I guess so," Laura says with a smile.

I hear Maria come rushing down the stairs and she calls out to her mother before making her way into the kitchen. I turn around in my chair to look at her, now fully dressed, and she looks to me like she had no idea I'd dropped by. "Reverend Doyle," she asks, "how long have you been here?"

"Not long," I say to her with a warm smile. "What about you," I ask her, "why aren't you at school?"

"Free period," she says.

"Free period," I say with a casual nod. "As long as you're using it to catch up with any schoolwork you've missed."

"Are you kidding me?" Laura chuckles and says, "Every time I see her in front of a computer, she's on Twitter or something like that."

"We're talking about homework assignments," Maria says right before she asks, "what's that smell? Have you been smoking?" and the question causes Laura to chuckle a little harder.

"You Leeson women," I say with a shake of my head, "keeping your little secrets…"

"Mom," Maria says, "I'm just heading over to the library to work on my book report."

"I hope that's the truth," Laura says, "because they give you free periods for the reason Reverend Doyle gave, not to sit in the mall gossiping about boys and music."

"I'm going the library," Maria says, "I'm not the one gossiping right now, am I?"

"She's got you," I say to Laura from behind a smile.

"Tell me about it," Laura says, "I don't know where she gets it from. Anyway," she says to her young daughter, "I want you home for dinner. That's five o'clock."

"I'll be back," Maria says and as she turns to leave she adds, "I'll see you soon, Reverend Doyle."

"Sure thing," I say back to her and then she's out of the front door and it's just me and her mother again.

"Kids," Laura says with a shake of her head. "They have no idea what the world is really like."

"Talking about bad things," I say, "Mitch warned me about Sam."

"Sam?"

"Sure," I say, "it *is* Sam Pennington, isn't it? Frequents a bar called Velma's?"

"Oh," Laura says with a smile. "I know who you mean."

"I hear she's sweet for a man in uniform," I say, hoping to stir a little trouble by having Laura assume everybody in town is talking about Sam's infatuation with the good reverend.

"She's certainly lonely," Laura says like it doesn't bother her in the slightest, "and that son of hers could test the patience of a saint. But I don't think she has any romantic feelings for Paul; people just like to make out she does. It's just," she struggles to explain, "she has nobody since her husband walked out on her and the only man she can think of to try and talk a little sense into her boy is Paul. But what kind of teenage rebel is going to sit down and listen to what the local reverend has to say?"

"Exactly. But her son," I ask, "is he in any of Maria's classes?"

"I don't think so," she says. "I don't think he even attends school any more. Sam works from early morning to mid-afternoon, so he just lazes around the house doing whatever he wants."

I ask, "Where is it she works again?"

"Sam? Over at the mini-market… right by the church. That's how she first noticed Paul."

"I bet it is," I smirk.

21

I LEAVE THE Leeson family home in good spirits and a few doors down, I drop my pace a little and take a look around me, half expecting Maria to step out from behind a tree or something where she's been waiting for me, but it doesn't happen. A little disappointed, I light up a cigarette and continue walking. Some guy easing his car back home following a visit to the grocery store throws a quizzical look in my direction and I smile at him and wave. He waves back, albeit a little reluctantly and brings the car to a stop outside his home. I carry on walking, carry on smiling and think about how Leeson will find out about my visit. Through his wife, his daughter, or confused neighbour?

It takes me a while but I eventually find myself right by Leeson's place of business again but I don't stop by for a visit; I keep walking, eyes open, looking for the *right* mini-market. And I find it easily enough, stroll on in and walk straight for the counter. There's a strong smell of bleach in the air, like maybe somebody recently spilled something in one of the aisles and a store attendant has just cleaned it up.

A young girl and a fat, older one with a hairy mole to the corner of her mouth are stood behind the counter; the fat one filing her nails, coloured a luminous orange, while the younger one turns one page after another of the glossy magazine she's holding in front of her. The magazine looks to focus on nothing other than the Kardashians, a family of nonentities whose very popularity escapes me without any difficulty whatsoever. But both women are joking and laughing, like they're not working at all, and they don't seem to notice me until I'm standing right in front of the counter. The older one looks me up and down, uses the gum she's chewing on to blow a bubble, before finally asking, "What can I do for you?"

Both girls are wearing nametags. The younger of the two is called CARRIE and the older of the two is called CANDICE.

I wonder if they're related solely for the fact both names begin with a C. "I'm here to speak with Sam," I reply.

"Sam?" Candice says back to me. The two exchange a brief glance and then Candice looks back to me as Carrie looks back to her magazine. A magazine that destroys a couple of brain cells with every passing second you're near it. "The delivery boy?"

"No," I tell her, "Sam Pennington."

Candice smiles to Carrie. Carrie smiles to Candice. Candice says to me in little more than an excited whisper, "You just hold on for one second." Candice turns around to a telephone hanging on the wall behind her, a telephone I hadn't even noticed until now, and Carrie gets to sniggering as she pretends to focus on her magazine. "Sam," Candice says down the receiver after a dozen or so seconds, "you have a gentleman caller out on the shop floor. Uh-huh. No, but I think you'll want to see him. Okay, bye-bye." Candice ends the call and says to me, "She's working out back, but she'll be out in a minute," and Carrie struggles to keep herself from laughing like she's just heard the funniest joke in the world for the first time.

"Where'll she be coming from?" I ask, realising there's no door behind the counter.

"Doors to the back are in the far corner over there," Candice says pointing over me. "You can go wait for her over there, if you'd like to have a more private conversation with her?"

"Thank you," I say, "that would be nice," and the two girls start laughing as soon as my back is turned, like I can't hear them just because I'm not looking at them. I ignore it, walk over to the sealed double doors with a sign over them saying STAFF ONLY BEYOND THIS POINT and as if the sign isn't enough, you have to punch in a key-code to get through the doors. Even the small window on each door has thick strips of plastic behind it, meaning you can't see into the back at all. But the door opens and a reasonably attractive, older woman with straw-coloured hair and black roots almost walks right into me. She's clearly surprised to find somebody waiting so close to the door. I smile at her, take a single step back, offering an apology and take a look at her nametag. It says SAM. She looks to me with mild confusion and asks me, "Can I help you, sir?"

I ask, "Sam Pennington?" noticing the gooseflesh on her arms and her erect nipples. I'd love to believe I'd caused such a reaction but I have to admit there's probably a lot of items kept refrigerated out back.

She waits a moment, like she's just checking she is indeed Sam Pennington, and finally nods her head. "Yes?"

"Reverend Doyle," I say, bringing a finger to my off-white collar. "I hear you're looking for a reverend's touch."

22

SAM COMES WALKING out of the store with a Styrofoam cup filled with coffee in each hand and sees me waiting for her on the nearest bench. She smiles and hands me one of the coffees. "Thanks," I say taking it from her. The heat of the drink is noticeable, as it always is when in one of these cheap containers.

"Not a problem," she says placing herself beside me, hand taking an open pack of Millbrook Lites from her pocket. "Cigarette?" she asks.

"I have my own," I say taking the pack and Zippo from my inner jacket pocket. "But thanks." We each light up in silence. There's a soft breeze to the air. You can even hear it because the cars on the road are easing along instead of rushing by like they will in the big cities.

A sudden gust of wind blows a little hair into Sam's eyes and she brushes it aside before asking me, "So what is it I can do for you?"

"Oh," I tell her, "I'm not here to ask for any favours… I'm not collecting for a new church roof or anything like that at all. I'm here to talk with you about your son."

"Danny?" she sighs. "What's he gone and done now?"

"Nothing," I laugh, "nothing at all. I just hear he's been causing you some trouble of late."

Sam rolls her eyes and says, "That's putting it lightly," before asking, "but who told you that, Reverend Leeson?"

"It doesn't matter who told me of your problem," I say with a wave of my hand, "just that somebody wants me to help out if I can. You do want a little help, don't you?"

Sam nods her head, bites down on her bottom lip for a moment. "Lord knows I need it," she says and I smile on dropping a hand on her shoulder and giving it a little squeeze.

"I can't promise you any miracles," I tell her, taking my hand back, "but I'm here to do my best, if you're sure you want my

86

best. But your boy," I say, "*Danny*… you think there's much of a chance he'll even listen to a man of God when he's going through a rebellious phase?"

She takes a drag on her cigarette and smiles, smoke drifting out between the gaps of her teeth as she looks back to the minimarket. The light shining on the large window stops me from getting a good look inside, but I'd bet Candice and Carrie are watching us both like hawks. "Well," she finally says, "I know he won't listen to me. And it's only me and him at home, you know? I was thinking it would be good for him to have a man sit and talk with him about the way he's behaving."

"Have you tried asking one of his teachers?"

Sam laughs at that one. "I can't get him to go to school," she says. "Try as I might, he just won't budge. Which is funny." She adds, "His not wanting to move is funny is what I mean, because I think it's this town that has him acting the way he is."

"What do you mean by that?" I ask out of a genuine interest.

"He just has it in his head that if you are born in a little town like this, you have no real chance of leaving. Just last year," she says, "he had all of these dreams of going to a college far away from here but then he just went and gave up on his studying and I'm talking almost overnight."

I glance at my cigarette to see how much of it is left before taking a quick drag on it. "Was he having any trouble with the kids at school?"

"No," she says, shaking her head. "He had a lot of friends and he had his dreams and then he just stepped away from them all." She wipes a tear away from her eye and laughs. "He has a guitar," she says like it means everything, "and he wants to become a big rock star and have homes all over the world."

"That's pretty normal."

"It is," she laughs again, "but he can't play it. He tried but he wasn't good at it right away so he stopped trying. He'll plug it in to the amplifier every once in a while," she says, "and strum at it real loud, but there's no rhythm. No notes, melody, nothing."

I say, "Like a lot of music recorded nowadays," and that has her laugh again. "What time are you going to be finished here for the day?"

"Just under an hour."

"You want me to meet you outside? Go back home with you and talk with Danny?"

Sam nods her head and smiles at me. "That'd be great," she says.

23

Sam takes us back to her place in her rusting blue Beetle which continuously sticks between the second and third gears. During the journey, I'm wondering if the girl has been horribly misjudged. To me, she comes across as a woman who cares deeply about her son and nothing more. I start to wonder if maybe, a little gossip caused by two morons like Candice and Carrie could have simply taken hold of the town without any real difficulty.

"This is my place," she says parking outside her two-storey home. It looks like a reasonably nice place; not as nice as Leeson's but still much nicer (and bigger) than the home I was raised in. It doesn't stand out like a sore thumb among the other houses on the road. In fact, it looks like Sam finds the time to climb up a ladder and clean out the gutters or apply a lick of paint whenever needed. It's either that or maybe she has a long list of lonely gentlemen all too happy to help her out…

"It looks nice," I tell her, "real homely. Is Danny going to be inside?"

"Let's go and find out," she says killing the engine. We climb out of the car and I follow her to the front door. She unlocks it and we step inside to the smell of various spices. "The slow cooker has been on all morning," she says in explanation, looking back to me with a smile. "It isn't like I can rely on Danny to make either of us something to eat."

"It smells great," I say following her into the kitchen where the smell increases tenfold and I spot the slow cooker shaking gently atop of the stove.

"You're welcome to have some," she says setting up two cups of instant coffee. "Just hold on for one second, would you? I'll go see if Danny is in his room." Sam walks out of the kitchen and I lean against the nearest worktop, listening to the sounds of her footsteps racing up the stairs as she calls his name. The footsteps move directly over me, fall silent for a while, and then I hear a toilet flush before Sam returns to the kitchen. "That boy," she says shaking her head, pouring freshly boiled water into the two waiting cups.

"I take it he isn't at home?"

Sam says, "He isn't home. I can't say I'm too surprised by that."

Maria Leeson immediately comes to mind so I ask, "Could he have gone over to the library?"

Sam laughs at that and apologises for doing so right away. "I'm sorry," she says, "but you clearly don't know my son! There is no chance at all he will be over at the library."

I nod once and decide to see just how much trust there is with the dog-collar I'm currently wearing. "Would you like me to go and take a look around his room?"

Sam quits stirring one of the coffees for a second and then raises her head to look at me. "Up the stairs," she sighs, "you'll know what room is his."

I nod once. "I'll be quick," I tell her.

"Take all the time you need."

The stairs creak under each step that I take, despite the old yet thick brown carpet that covers them. The landing at the top of them is pretty dark and I get the feeling you only get more than enough light on it if you happen to leave every door up here wide open. And I notice how one door stands ajar with a movie poster for Rob Zombie's Halloween sequel sticking to it. I contemplate snooping around, looking around Sam's room for handcuffs and spray-cream first, but decide against it. I simply push the door to Danny's room open and find myself being greeted by the musky, sweaty smell that inhabits the room of many a teenage boy. It's difficult to see the carpet for all the black clothing on the floor, but I immediately spot the electric guitar, covered in stickers leaning against his bed. One look at the covers on his bed stops me from reaching for it; they look greasy and old. There are plenty of posters up on the wall and, unlike the posters on Maria Leeson's walls, they have been put up lopsided.

I'm taking it all in when I notice a picture of Tony Warr, but it's not just any picture, it's an enlarged picture of him wearing a slutty nurse's uniform and holding a filthy syringe out for all to see. The very first picture I ever saw of him, as shown to me by the real Reverend Doyle. My eyes won't leave it, despite the crushing feeling that's growing inside of me. I feel close to tears just for looking at it this long. It's the thought of lighting a cigarette that pulls me away from the poster, because I soon realise the potential fire hazard surrounding me.

"Oh, Doyle," I sigh on looking away, my gaze returning to the floor. I look for a sign, any sign, that Danny has screwed Maria Leeson in this very room… an abandoned bra, a soiled condom, anything. But all I see around me is waste. I turn to leave but stop on noticing his CD collection neatly stored, alphabetically on a tall rack carefully screwed to the wall. …And You Will Know Us By The Trail of Dead, Anthrax, The Black Keys, David Bowie, Boxing Hares, Alice Cooper... It goes on and on. I read every spine ranging from ...And You Will Know Us By The Trail of Dead to Zombina and the Skeletones and must only recognise a quarter or so of the names.

In the end, it's the overwhelming urge to light a cigarette that has me making my way back down the stairs, hoping my coffee hasn't turned cold as stone during my absence.

"You find anything?" Sam asks me, leaning against a worktop with both hands around her cup.

"It looks like you have a teenage boy living here," I reply and that makes her smile. Reaching for my cigarettes I ask her, "You mind if I smoke?"

"Not at all," she says.

"You want one?"

"I have this," she says, reaching to the side of her to hold up one of those electronic cigarettes you see a lot of people with nowadays. "I smoke it when I'm inside the house."

"So you don't stink the place out? You should have told me," I tell her, "I'll gladly go and smoke outside."

"It's nothing like that," she smiles. "You have to recharge these things a lot; it makes sense to only smoke them when you're close to the mains."

24

Danny hasn't returned yet but Sam has taken to dishing out the dinner. Dinner I've agreed to stay for. I have two reasons for accepting her offer, one being it's a free meal and the other being how I'm curious to see if her son will return with Maria Leeson in tow. "You often eat alone?" I ask.

"More often than not," Sam says and then she hands me a knife and fork before sitting down. "Dig in," she says and she stabs a cut of spiced meat with her knife before saying, "my goodness, we haven't said grace!"

"Don't worry about it," I say to her with a smile.

"No," she says, lowering her cutlery, "you must think I'm terribly rude, and I'm sorry. Please," she says placing her hands together and bowing her head, "take the floor."

I smile, bow my head and begin with the Lord's Prayer, or what I remember to be the Lord's Prayer.

"Our Father, who art in heaven,
Hallowed by thy name, thy Kingdom come,
Thy will be done on Earth, as it is in Heaven,
Give us this day our daily bread,
And forgive us our debts, as we forgive our debtors,
And lead us not into temptation but deliver us from evil,
For thine is the Kingdom, the power and the glory,
Forever and ever. Amen."

"Amen," Sam repeats with a smile and then we finally begin our meal. "You know I've never heard it that way before? I mean the part about forgiving debts. I was taught *trespasses*."

"It's the way it was taught to me," I tell her without letting her know it was a sadistic uncle who taught me it that way.

The food that had been slowly cooking itself throughout the day tastes real good. Too many people rely on microwaves and ready-meals these days. I guess I'd live on all that processed shit myself, if I was out at work from nine until five and had no time to prepare a meal on getting back, but I'd rather not. Not that I'm a real connoisseur or anything like that; I've lived on breakfast cereal, sandwiches and greasy diner meals for most of my life, but I got the impression that a lot of the shit they served us inside was processed and so I'd rather not go back to it.

Sam nods, looks at me and asks, "Would you like a drink to go with your dinner?" Right away, I'm wondering if she's going to suggest a little wine… Something to loosen the off-white collar a little if she's real lucky. I flash her my best toothy grin on hoping she's about to reveal herself to be the real temptress and ask, "What have you got?"

"Fruit punch," she says, "water, milk…"

"I'll have what you're having," I reply and so she pours us both a glass of fruit juice from a carton she takes from the refrigerator. It's so cold I can't even detect a taste, but it's orange in colour, I can tell you that much.

We finish our meal and I stand nearby with a cigarette while she cleans the dishes. Danny is still to return. I ask her, "So does your son have a usual time for coming back home?"

"Usually sometime between ten and eleven," she says with a tired-sounding sigh. "I'm usually up in my room, watching Leno, when he comes back. He'll have his supper and head straight for his room and listen to his music really loud until I tell him to put on his damn headphones. Sorry for cursing."

"Forget about it," I smirk. "But what about you?" I ask, "Don't you ever cut loose?"

"I don't know," she laughs. "I go to a bar called Velma's maybe once or twice a week, but that's only when Danny has been acting up a little worse than usual. I go see if a band is playing, have a couple of drinks and come back home."

"You like music?"

"Love it," she says. "I wanted to be a music journalist when I was growing up but you know how it is, things can distract you if you're not too careful. But listen to me! Look at you, a reverend and still looking so young! How old were you when you knew that's exactly what you wanted to be… a reverend, I mean?"

"I don't know," I tell her. "What a lot of it came down to," I claim, "is how nervous I got around the opposite sex."

"A strapping boy like you?" she laughs. "What did you have to be nervous about?"

"I don't know," I smile, certain I've struck gold now we're here. "I just get - or *got* - a little nervous around beautiful women. If it wasn't for this collar I'm wearing, I'd be stumbling all over my words for trying to talk with you right now."

Sam laughs at that one, like it's made her week or something. "Believe me," she says brushing her hair back, "you've no reason to be nervous around women. You could have had them eating out of the palm of your hand."

"I don't know about that. But anyway- *music*. You have any good records?"

"I have records I like," she smiles. "The stereo in the living room plays CDs and vinyl records. Not that Danny appreciates anything like that these days," she says. "I can't remember the last time he went out and bought a record, he downloads them all right onto his computer now."

"It sounds like you really appreciate your records," I say to pull the conversation back away from her son. "You feel like listening to some?"

She looks back at me and laughs. "Now?" she asks in surprise.

"Why not? I'm only staying in town for a matter of days," I tell her, "and it would be fun to get a bit of excitement out of it. A little drink, a little dancing… You do have something we can drink, don't you?"

"Sure," she laughs, "a couple bottles of spirits Danny has probably been watering down since God only knows when, but we should have enough to enjoy ourselves."

25

THERE'S AN ELECTRIC light burning away behind the closed curtains of room four at the Four Card motel and an expensive-looking 4X4 parked right outside my room. It's dark, it's late, it's cold and I'm a little merry from drinking and dancing with Sam Pennington but I stop to look the vehicle over regardless, like looking at it will make me forget the disappointment I'm feeling about how Sam didn't try getting fresh with me when she had the chance and I had to settle for a neighbour seeing me leave her place so late. I take a step back delving a hand inside my pocket for my cigarettes and continue staring at the 4X4, wondering who could afford such a ride and still decide to spend time in a dump like the Four Card.

I'm lighting my cigarette when my question is answered. The door to room four opens and a youngish guy steps out and looks at me. His glasses look like a girl should be wearing them and despite the cold and his bony frame, he's wearing a short-sleeved T-shirt. "Nice car," I tell him. "This yours?"

"Yeah," he says and he cautiously takes a step out of the door. Noticing my dog collar, he relaxes and steps out a little more but with some confidence this time. "I've had that a year, a year and a half tops. I'm thinking of selling it, getting something a little sportier."

"Roads are pretty good around here," I grin. "It's not like you have much use for an all terrain vehicle, is it?"

"I suppose not," he says and then he's quiet for a second. "You staying near here?" he asks.

"Room three," I say pointing over at my door. "I reckon I'll be here a week at least and then I'll make tracks."

"Good to have a plan," he nods. "Is your room as nasty as mine?"

"Nastier, I'm betting. I think I only got it because the manager happened to be holding the key for it."

"Same here," he laughs.

I take a quick step towards him and he jumps back a little without knowing he was going to, so I slow right down and offer him my hand. "Name's Doyle," I tell him.

"Jack," he says and I get the impression he smells the alcohol on me. "You had a good night?"

"Could have been better," I tell him. "*Should* have been better, even."

"Story of the world," he says.

"Tell me about it," I say in understanding. "You want a smoke?" I ask him, holding the open pack out for him.

"Sure," he says and he extracts a cigarette and lights it using his own plastic lighter. "Thanks. This is quite a sleepy little town, isn't it?"

"Sure is," I agree.

"You sent here for work?"

"Me?" I smile and say to him, "Don't let the collar at my throat fool you any. Man in my line of work would gladly don a turban or a skullcap if he would benefit from it."

"That's funny," he laughs. "What *is* your line of work?"

"Truth be told, I'm in-between-jobs at the moment."

"Right," he smiles. "That's the economy for you, isn't it?"

"Amen to that."

"Amen," he laughs and then he looks me up and down and he asks, "do you get high?"

"Sure," I answer with a slow nod. "I get high."

Jack nods this time. "I got some real good green in my room," he says. "I was rolling a fat one right before I noticed you. You want to come in and get stoned? I've got my iPod already set up in its docking station and everything. The speakers are good enough," he adds.

"Sure," I smile and I drop my cigarette to the floor and step on it. "It's the best offer I've had since arriving here."

"Pissy little town like this," Jack says, turning back to his room, "it's a real miracle of an offer. Come on in."

I follow him into his room and it's almost identical to mine, right down to the smell. As he closes the door behind me I notice he's pulled one of the drawers right out of the bedside dresser and placed it on the floor to use in place of an ashtray. There's a bottle of Sailor Jerry's lying on the bed, unopened. The bathroom door stands wide open with the light on but there's nobody in there. "Take a seat," he says, "if you can find anyplace."

"Thanks," I say and I sit on my haunches near the end of the bed with my back to the wall because it's close enough to the bedside drawer for my liking. Jack heads to the top of the bed and lifts a pillow to reveal the joint he had been busy rolling. He's finishing the job in no time at all.

"The bathroom is the fucking worst," he says. "You should see the mould growing up one of the walls. It looks like it could be fucking breathing."

"Have you tried licking it?"

Jack throws me a quizzical look. "No," he says, "what makes you say that?"

"There's a slim chance it has hallucinogenic properties."

"Get out of here," he says.

"I'm serious," I tell him. "Chances are one of us will give it a try before the night is out."

"Right," he smirks, "you're just trying to get me to lick fungus," and he leans over the side of the bed to where his iPod is docked and he presses a button to start the music. Just like he'd claimed, the speakers are pretty good… I recognise the Sneaker Pimps right away. "I've put it on random," he says, "so we could be in for a real trippy night," and then he starts laughing.

26

I'm part awake but I'm mostly asleep and I can hear this tapping, like I'm in my casket and somebody is bringing their knuckles down against the closed lid. And it's that very thought that understandably brings me back to full consciousness.

I'm flat out on my bed in the Four Card motel, fully clothed and suffering from a hangover. My throat is like dry ice and there's a bad taste in my mouth. I can smell the alcohol that remains on my breath. Running a hand over my mouth, I detect the smell of cigarette smoke and grass on my sleeve. And I'm exhausted… exhausted as hell.

There's another knock at my door. I swing my legs onto the floor and stand, only for a moment, before dropping back onto my ass. Taking a deep breath to prepare myself, I get back onto my feet and stay on them this time around.

And then somebody is knocking at my door all over again.

"Just a second," I say on staggering to the door. The chain is in place. My shoes are beside the door but I'm still in my socks. "Just a second," I say again, freeing the chain and pulling the bolts out of place. I open the door and the morning sun burns my tender eyes.

Leeson is standing with his back to the door, like he had been walking away but heard me at the last possible second. He turns, slowly, to face me. He's wearing expensive sunglasses, far too expensive for a small town reverend to pull off, and I see my reflection, clear as day, in the lenses. Looking at Leeson, I only see myself for a moment. And this is all so unexpected…

"Reverend Leeson," I say to him and my voice sounds like my throat feels. "This is a surprise… What can I do you for?"

"You can accompany me to some light breakfast," he says.

I nod and rub the delicate stones of sleep from the corner of my eyes. "What time is it?"

"A little after nine-thirty," he says. "If you don't think you're up to eating," he says, "I'll shout you a coffee."

I nod in understanding. "You want to step inside a moment?" I ask without knowing I was going to.

"I'll wait out here," he says and then he turns his back to me. I smirk, close the door with a soft click and walk into the bathroom. I pull at the switch and the room is soon a lot brighter, but it's all artificial. My reflection stares back at me from the cloudy mirror hanging above the sink and I see the black specks dotted around my chin, mouth, cheek. I could easily bet my last dollar I got the marks on my face from licking at the mould in Jack's bathroom but I have no recollection of doing so. And I smile a little wider on wondering what Leeson made of the dirt on my face.

"Paul Leeson," I chuckle as I splash a little hot water towards my mouth. There's an old facial cloth on the floor, probably as old as the room itself, but I use it to dry my skin off anyway before making my way to the door. Slipping on my shoes, I find the keys to the room in my left shoe and chuckle one last time. Stepping out onto the street, I see Leeson admiring the 4X4.

"This yours?"

"I wish," I say on closing the door behind me. I check it's locked and it is. "Belongs to the guy in four."

Leeson nods. "You know him?"

"Can't say so," I shrug. "Where is it you want to go for coffee?"

"Little place nearby. Let's go," he says and he starts leading the way knowing I'll fall in beside him soon enough. I haven't been at his side for more than eight seconds before he starts talking again. "How're you finding Whicker?" he asks me.

"Not too different from the small place I grew up in," I taunt him.

"Really," he says and I think he's going to ask me for a name but instead he asks me, "and how long do you think you'll be here for?"

"I don't know," I shrug. "Until I've done what I'm here to do."

"I thought you were needed farther north?"

"Men like us," I say, "we're needed in a lot of places… Especially when the young and the innocent are concerned, am I right?"

"Right," he says but it doesn't sound like he means it. It sounds like I could be saying anything at all but he's only paying attention to his own private thoughts, a part of him listening out for a certain word or phrase but that's about it.

I take the pack of cigarettes from my pocket and see there are only four left. "You want a cigarette?" I ask like a good Christian would.

"No," Leeson says, "thank you."

"Suit yourself," I tell him and I light up before talking again. "We any closer to this coffee place of yours?"

"Just around this upcoming corner," he says.

"So your name's Paul?" I smirk.

"Sure," he says.

"Like McCartney?"

"Same spelling but I can't tell you if I was named after him."

"You didn't know your parents too well?"

"No," he says, "did you?"

I laugh. "Are you asking me how well I knew your parents?"

We follow the curve in the road and the cafe he wants to get to comes into sight. "There it is," Leeson says to me, like he didn't even hear what I just asked him.

27

THE CAFE IS nothing like the waffle house I accompanied the Leeson family to; it's clearly a place meant for attracting a whole different type of customer… The wealthy members of Whicker society made up of a talented surgeon or two or something like that. Or maybe the town's wealthiest only reside here for the peace and quiet and commute to work every morning but at least they have here to stop by once or twice a day, I wouldn't know, but the place doesn't just *look* expensive, it *smells* expensive. Seriously, the coffee I smell, following the good reverend into the place must be brewed using the rarest beans of the rarest rainforest and *that* is why Leeson and I are the only customers when we walk on in.

"You want a decaf," Leeson asks me, finally removing his sunglasses, "or an ordinary coffee or something special? If it is made using coffee beans," he boasts, "they'll make it for you right here."

"Get me whatever you're having."

"No problem," he says, "take a seat but make sure it isn't a booth. Those are reserved for parties of three or more."

"Like more than three people are going to come to this place," I say, heading to a two-seater table but Leeson acts like he didn't hear me and walks over to the counter. I glance over every table and booth in search of a forgotten newspaper but I have no luck in catching sight of one. Place like this probably takes the abandoned newspapers and keeps them behind the counter… lets you read them for a fraction of the retail price.

Leeson walks over to the table and sits opposite me. I continue looking over to the nearest window for a little while but eventually turn to face him. He's already looking at me. "This your first time here?" he asks me after we've been looking into one another's eyes for a second or two.

"You mean *here*," I ask him, pressing a finger down on the

table top, "or Whicker?"

Leeson grins. "This is your first time in Whicker," he tells me, "I know that much. I was just wondering if you'd stopped by this place yet."

"No," I say with a shake of my head, "and even if I had done, I'd have walked in and walked straight back out again."

"Yeah?" He asks, "What makes you say that?"

"It's cold," I answer him with a shrug of my shoulders. "It's all style over substance. I thought a man in your profession would know the importance of making a place feel warm and inviting."

A young waitress comes over carrying a black tray above her shoulder and lowers it once she's near enough to unload the two cappuccinos and lay them down on the table in front of us. "Two cappuccinos," she says to Leeson. "Would you like to order anything else?"

Leeson keeps his eyes locked on me as he asks, "You hungry? I said I'd shout you breakfast."

"So you did," I say to him with a smile. "What would you recommend?"

Leeson looks to the waitress and says, "Get him a plate of scrambled eggs over toast with sausages and mushrooms. Hold the beans."

"Coming right up," she says before walking back to the preparation area.

"Aren't you hungry?"

"No," he says, shaking his head, "had a good breakfast before leaving this morning. Thank you for the flowers, by the way," he adds, dragging his cappuccino towards him.

"Just my way of thanking you all. Mitch has given me quite the deal over at his motel."

"Yeah," Leeson sighs, "he filled me in this morning. I dropped by to see him before knocking at your door," he says. "Mitch told me he saw you staggering out of room four last night, looking a little intoxicated."

"That's probably true. I was drinking rum with the new guy staying there."

Leeson leans back in his chair and asks, "I thought you didn't know him?"

"I don't. I met him for the first time when I was coming back last night and he doesn't know anybody in town so he invited me in for a couple of drinks. He needed somebody to talk with," I say with a weary sigh, "and the collar we wear makes people feel comfortable around us. Well," I smile, "the collar *I* wear. I can't help but notice yours is still missing."

"People around town know me," Leeson says, "know what it is I stand for. And some of the people," he continues, "have already started asking about you."

I smile at him. "Asking what?"

"Are you here on official business," he says. "Are you in the business of making house calls, because a couple of people know all about you visiting Sam Pennington at work and going back to her place until late. I have no idea how many people could take to thinking we're working together but some, Mitch included, already want to know if I personally will vouch for you."

"And will you? We're of the same cloth," I say on bringing my finger against the off-white collar I'm wearing, "and that would make us brothers, wouldn't it?"

"I wouldn't know about that. What did you say the name of your church was again?"

"Forget about it," I tell him, "a small-town reverend like you wouldn't want to go looking around Los Angeles because you'd never find your way back here." I take a deep breath like I'm about to yawn but say, "I guess I did all of my growing up out in Los Angeles. That's where I landed after leaving home. Home," I smirk, "what a laugh. Homes are supposed to be comforting and bursting with warm memories, but I didn't have any of that."

"Me neither," Leeson says like he wants me to know he isn't a sucker for a sob story.

"You see this scar here?" I ask, holding my left palm out for him to see. He looks at it for the most fleeting of moments before his eyes fall back on mine. "Most folk carry a treasured photograph around to remind them of home. I carry this scar."

"I can't say my upbringing was any better."

"But you left as soon as you could; didn't you? Sure you did. You ever wonder how that was for the people you left behind?"

Leeson brings his drink to his mouth. "I didn't leave anybody behind," he says.

"We all leave somebody behind. Even me," I smirk. "I left a vicious, old son of a bitch behind. After enough drinking, he probably went and asked God how he ever could have raised two boys so badly. But you grew up in a home, didn't you? You ever wonder if that will have had an impact on your way with people? This town," I say with a shake of my head, "looking to you for guidance when you struggled to find it for yourself."

Leeson takes a deep breath like he's about to yawn but only asks, "What is it that's stopping you from moving on… What're you here for?"

"To get what's owed to me," I reply. That's what I want more than anything; an apology from him. I'd walk away from this place without causing any long-lasting damage if he'd just give me that.

"Here's your order," the waitress announces, returning to our table with the breakfast Leeson selected for me. She places it down in front of me and I have to admit, it looks and smells pretty special. "Is there anything else I can get for you?"

"I think that should do it," Leeson smiles to her like we're all friends. "Could you do me a favour and put that on my tab? It's just that I've got to leave about now."

"Sure," she says back to him with a smile, "I'll make a note about it right away."

"Thanks," he says to her, still smiling, as she retreats one last time.

I gently place a napkin over my lap on saying, "Maybe I'll see you a little later."

"Maybe," he says back to me on standing to leave.

28

I WALK AROUND the town for a while but find nothing to keep a firm hold of my attention. The people I pass by seem real friendly and say hello but they are few and far between, like the majority are at work or school, so in the end I head back to the Four Card. Jack's 4X4 isn't parked outside, so I don't bother knocking at room four. I head straight into my room and kick off my shoes while locking the door behind me. I notice a hole in the sole of the left one, meaning my foot is bound to get wet next time it rains but there's nothing I can do about that right now. I just drop onto the bed and look at the ceiling for a while before closing my eyes.

I dream that I'm looking at a reptile tank and there's a snake inside but it isn't like any snake you would see in real life; it's covered in long fur so you don't see an inch of skin and sharp hooks, bones, I'd bet are sticking out of it here and there. If that isn't a warning to keep you from touching it, I don't know what is. Suddenly, I'm outside a college on a real nice day. A lot of students are just hanging around, making the most of the bright sun before returning to class, but I rush over to a small building like I've got to find somebody real bad. It turns out I'm looking for an incredibly beautiful girl and I find her behind the building. Laughing, she opens her clasped hands and flicks her wrist. A white butterfly flutters away from her open hands and her friend, standing a couple of feet away from her, tenderly catches the butterfly in her own hands and the girls start laughing.

I try talking to the most beautiful of the two girls but she quickly walks away with her friend in tow. I follow them, trying to earn their trust and attention, but soon there are a bunch of jocks behind me saying the usual shit about *great tits* and *checking out asses*. I start jumping backwards, trying to bring the back of my head into the ringleader's nose, but I keep missing. I'm doing all of this while trying to stay close to the girls and the jocks carry on following close behind me despite my blatant attacks.

I wake up and I'm on my side, facing the open bathroom door. The available light has me assume it's nearing sunset. I sit, scratch the back of my neck and head to the door, unlocking it before looking outside. The 4X4 is back so I wonder if it was hearing Jack return to his room that woke me. I look up and down the street but see nothing worthwhile. I scratch the back of my neck again, light a cigarette and step outside to knock at room four. The curtain twitches slightly as Jack takes a look outside before opening up. "Doyle," he says to me with a smile, "how're things?"

"Slow. You been up to much?"

"Me?" He shakes his head and says, "Nah. Why do you ask?"

"No reason," I tell him. "You feel like a beer? We can go to a bar or we can buy a crate and bring them back here."

"Sure," he grins, "I could go for a beer. You want to leave now?"

"Give me a half hour," I tell him, "I need to take a shower before we leave."

"No problem. You want me to call for you or are you coming back here?"

"I'll come back here," I say, turning back to my room, "I won't be too long."

"I'll be waiting."

29

I TAKE JACK over to Velma's bar and despite how he insists on cracking funnies along the way, I can't help but notice that he seems a little nervous to be so far away from his room. If a car heading in our direction takes to slowing down, he'll take a real long look at the driver before finishing what it was he was saying. I want to ask him about it but I don't, just in case he thinks I'm being a little intrusive but once we're back indoors, he seems happy again. "Is that a mechanical bull?" he asks as we're heading for the bar.

"Sure is," I tell him reaching for my wallet. "Thing even works. But what're you having?"

"Let me get them," he says as the bartender approaches and I'm about to ask him if he's sure when I notice just how thick the wallet he's keeping out of the barman's sight is. He asks me, "What do you want?"

"A beer," I say, "or whatever you're drinking."

"Two bottles of Bud and two shots of Sambuca," Jack says to the barman and then he turns back to talk with me as the barman sets up our drinks. "So is this the best place in town to drink?"

"I don't know," I confess. "It's the only bar anybody has told me about."

"It's the best bar," the barman says on sliding our drinks out in front of us. "Everyplace else is filled with posers."

"You have those here?" Jack smirks, paying the man. If the employee had taken offense at Jack's remark, he soon loses it on being given a five dollar tip. "You want to sit at a table?" he asks me once we've knocked back our Sambucas.

"Sure," I say with the heat of strong alcohol lingering on my breath, "there's one right over there."

We sit at a table that gives us a real good view of the place. Nobody can come in or out without our seeing them first. I know I'll be keeping my eyes open for Sam but I have no idea who Jack is looking out for. "To new experiences," he says.

"To new experiences," I say back to him and we clink our bottle necks together. "You know I met a writer last time I was in here?"

"No," Jack says. "What did he write?"

"I don't know," I shrug, "but it made him money."

"There are easier ways than writing," Jack says to me. "Dangerous, but easy."

"Tell me about it," I chuckle.

"Yeah," Jack smiles, "and then there was you… What is it you do to make ends meet?"

"This and that," I say with a shrug. "Mostly lifting what I need from here and there."

"And nobody suspects the man of God, am I right?"

"You're right," I nod.

"Man," he laughs, "I'll have to try that one out for myself."

"And what about you," I ask him, "what is it you do?"

"Drug dealer," he says like it's no big deal but I don't know whether I should believe him or not. Drug dealers always look big and nasty when they're shown on the TV but Jack is just about as thin as you can get without being rushed to hospital. And the feminine glasses he wears hardly do him any favours.

"You serious?"

"Yeah," he says with a nod.

"So what do you deal?"

"Whatever people want," he grins. "Ecstasy, coke, Molly, LSD, speed. But I draw the line at heroin," he says. "Sure, you get to know some real assholes when you're selling coke, but heroin is a whole different ballgame. I don't want to be around *those* people."

"No," I say, "I don't blame you… But what're you doing here?" I ask, "Are you on your way to collect from a nearby town or something?"

"Nothing like that," Jack says with a smile. "I'm just here for the peace and quiet." Of course, his story changes after a few more drinks. "Guy I was selling to," he explains, "out in a small part of Texas-"

"That's where you're from," I interrupt him, "Texas?"

"Not too far from there," Jack says, "but not originally. But anyway," he continues, "he was a good enough guy, never tried any shit or anything like that, but one of his friends got done for murder."

"Holy shit," I say.

"Tell me about it," Jack says in understanding. "But this guy, the one that was jailed for murder, was something of a role model in the town, so you can imagine the fuss that was kicked up once people found out what he had been accused of. It was found out one way or another that the guy I was selling to was pretty good friends with the killer in question, so everybody took to paying him extra attention. When it was found out he was a user of anything he could lay his hands on," Jack says on shaking his head from side to side, "things got tricky for me."

"I'll bet."

"It's real hard to move your stuff when you have all kinds of cops watching you," he says, "and you had better believe that they were watching me. Every lawman in Texas wanted to catch the next person who even sneezed wrong seeing how they'd let a man who would be jailed for murder look like a model citizen for so long."

I smile, expecting Jack to reveal how he was arrested for possession and now he's skipped the state. I go to tell him we have something in common but it turns out I'm way off the mark on this one.

"So for various reasons I won't bore you with, I dropped the ball and some people lost some money and now my name doesn't mean too much."

"Jesus," I mutter. "So what, you're in hiding because if they catch up with you, there'll be a gangland execution making it into the papers?"

"Nah," Jack laughs, picking up his beer. "It won't be nothing like that. I'm looking at a bit of a beating and some stern words, but I've never been too good at taking beatings," he grins at me. "My plan is to stay out of sight until it's all forgotten about."

"How long will that be?"

"In my line of business," he says, "no time at all. I'm serious. It's one of those funny situations… Even the *big* names haven't openly said they want somebody to teach me a quick lesson, but a lot of people will be hoping they'll get noticed if they're first to take a hold of me and throw a couple of kicks and punches. It's all something over nothing. I mean," he grins, "I even saw to it that the lost money was replaced before making my exit."

"If you're certain…"

"I am," Jack says, still grinning. "It'll be old news by the end of the week and people will be missing me because of the money I bring back to them."

"Man," I say, "I don't know how you can live like that."

"It's easy. I earned a lot of trust and I lost a little of it recently down to reasons out of my control, but it all comes right again in the end. It's not like I've screwed anybody over or killed somebody. Like I said," he shrugs, "something over nothing that'll soon be forgotten about."

30

WHEN WE COME to decide we'll have one more before making tracks, I insist on paying for them because Jack got the rest. "If you're sure," he says, "and see if you can get the bartender to call us a cab or something while you're there."

"You don't feel up to walking back?"

"Too far," Jack says with a shake of his head, "and I don't want to be running down alleyways to take a leak every five minutes when a ride could have us back at the motel in no time at all."

I wonder if he really wants to catch a cab because he's a little nervous, what with having told me his real reason for being in Whicker and drinking as he did so, but I don't try and put his mind at ease in case I offend him or in case I've got it all wrong. So I nod my head and say, "Sure," before making my way to the bar.

"Hey," a young barman who must have only just started his shift says to me. "What can I get you, padre?"

"Two bottles of Bud," I answer him, opening my wallet, and I'm surprised a moth doesn't flutter out. "And could you call a cab for me and my friend?"

"I'm sorry," he says, "but we're not allowed to use the phone behind the bar for stuff like that. There's a payphone just over there," he adds pointing to a payphone mounted to one of the far walls.

"Thanks," I tell him, walking over to the payphone, drunk enough to temporarily forget all about the beers I just asked for. There's a card for the local taxi firm stuck to the wall beside the payphone. I drop a little loose change into the slot and dial the number.

"Whicker Wheels," somebody says to me from down the line, "how may I help you?"

"Hello," I say. "I'd like a cab sent to Velma's bar."

"That's not a problem. Would you like a people carrier?"

"If you insist," I reply, "but there's only the two of us."

"I'll have a car sent out to you as soon as I can," the voice says, trying not to laugh at me. "Can I take your name so the driver knows who he is collecting?"

"Sure," I say. "It's Doyle... Reverend Doyle."

"I'll dispatch a car right away."

"Thanks," I say before hanging up. I take a step back, look around me for my beers and remember how I left them over at the bar, unpaid for. I head back over to find the barman looking at me, a smug grin on his face and two open bottles of Bud waiting in front of him. "Sorry about that," I tell him taking a twenty from my wallet. "Here you go."

"Thanks," he says and because I didn't tell him he could take a tip, he stands with the change in his hand and tries to strike up a conversation, probably hoping I'll tell him to take something just to get away from him. "So you're the mystery reverend I've heard a few people talking about?"

"That's me," I say, nodding offering him my hand with hopes he'll accept it and accidentally hand me my change on doing so, but he's smarter than that. He shakes with the other hand. "I'm Reverend Doyle."

"Pleasure to meet you," he says, "I'm Dwight."

"You been working here long, Dwight?"

"I guess so," he says, "almost a year."

"A year," I nod. "You know Sam?"

"Sam?"

"Sam Pennington."

"Oh," he says, "sure. I know Sam. She's in here from time to time."

"You know if she'll be here tonight?"

"I don't know," he says.

"Shame, she's a real piece of ass, isn't she?"

"I guess," he sniggers.

"I know I would," I smile. "Anyway," I ask him, "you know Reverend Leeson?"

"Paul? Sure," he says, "not from the church or anything, just from around town. He used to coach my little brother's baseball team."

"What about the Leeson women? That Maria," I smirk, "she's going to be quite a peach in no time at all, isn't she? Girl's near enough ripe already."

Dwight looks at me like maybe I'm about to say I was joking but he doesn't know if he'd find it funny even if I was. Truth be told, he looks damn uncomfortable and the change of mine he's holding is clearly getting to be real heavy. "Sure," he says, "if you reckon."

"Come on," I challenge him, "you really expect me to believe you haven't noticed?"

"I can't say I see them that much," he says. "But anyway, here's your change."

I take the money but keep a hold of his hand for a little while, just to keep him here. It's not like he has anybody else to serve, anyway. "When you're in a tiny little town like this one," I say, "I'm willing to bet you run out of options real fast... I bet you look to the potential candidates and check your watch, try to figure out if it's their time yet or if you'll be looking at the inside of a jail cell for sampling the goods too soon. Am I right," I ask, "am I right?"

"Listen," Dwight says on throwing his thumb back, "it's been real good talking with you but I have to go down into the cellar... A barrel needs replacing."

"No problem," I smile at him. "Just remember what I said. I'm a man of the world," I add. "You'd be surprised how wet this collar makes the ladies, so you let me know if you ever need any advice or to make a confession."

I wink at him and turn to head back to Jack. He's rolling a cigarette between his thumb and finger and every once in a while he sucks at the end but it doesn't light up because he clearly hasn't taken a match to it. Man must be suffering from some real bad nicotine cravings but isn't willing to light up in case the taxi driver arrives and tells him to lose it. "Here's your beer," I say, placing a bottle down in front of him as I lower myself back down into my chair.

"Thanks. You order a cab?"

"Sure," I nod. "I had to go over to the payphone because the bar-staff aren't allowed to use the phone behind the bar for that."

"I thought that's what you were doing," he grins. "Either that or calling a girl to see if she's home," he laughs and then sucks away at the end of his cigarette again.

"You can light that," I say, "worst case scenario is you might have to rip the end off when the cab arrives."

"I'm okay," he insists. "I can wait until we're back at the Four Card."

"Maybe," I say. "You ever consider smoking one of those electronic cigarettes?"

Jack shakes his head from side to side. "Not once," he says. "You have a rough idea to the shit that's in these," he says on holding his cigarette in front of my eyes, "but not in those electric kind. They're too new," he says, "too untested."

"You know what I read? I read if tobacco had only been discovered recently, they wouldn't be able to legalise it in any sense because it's that dangerous."

"I can believe that," Jack says on bringing the cigarette back to his lips. "But still," he sighs, "it still feels good, even after all this time."

"You should try lighting them every once in a while," I joke.

Jack laughs and knocks back a little beer. "What was going on with the bartender, anyway? It looked like things were getting a little uncomfortable over there."

"It's nothing," I smirk. "I don't know if I should tell you," I add and looking down at the table, I notice a beer-mat and suddenly remember the hole in my left shoe and wonder if I've found a way to keep my foot dry come rain or shine.

"Now you've *got* to," he laughs. "Come on," he says, "we're the only friends we have in this dump!"

"Okay," I nod, "okay. You know the local reverend?"

Jack shakes his head. "No," he says.

"Well," I tell him anyway, "his name's Leeson and I knew him a couple of years back."

"You knew him through the church or something?"

"Grew up in the same town," is all I'm willing to give away, "but he doesn't recognise me. I don't blame him," I say, "because I wouldn't recognise me. I've changed a heck of a lot."

"Let me guess," Jack grins, "before you found God, there was a girl you really liked and this Leeson took her from you?"

"It's nothing that interesting," I claim, "but I don't like him. I don't like him and I know he'll still be in Whicker long after I'm gone, so I want to leave him with a reminder of me this time around… Something he'll never be able to shake off, something he may never be able to work out and even if he can, he won't ever dare admit to it."

Jack laughs. "Sounds like a vendetta against a man of the cloth."

"I guess it is," I agree. "But I want to blacken his reputation and everything he's ever touched… I want to leave him so fucking broken…" I spit.

"Seeing as there's no girl involved," Jack snorts, "I'm surprised to hear how much of a problem you have with him."

"Yeah," I grin right as an idea hits me. "Listen," I ask, "you don't happen to have any coke on you, do you?"

"No," Jack laughs, "only a little green you're welcome to have with me once we're back at the motel."

"It isn't for me," I explain, "it's for the motel owner."

"If you're trying to get some money taken off of your bill," Jack smirks, "it won't quite work out if you're trying to bribe him with coke."

"It's nothing like that," I say before knocking back a little beer. "I was told the guy used to have a serious problem until Leeson helped him get over it."

"So you want to get him back on it?" Jack laughs and says, "That's ice cold! But seriously," he continues, "I'm bored out of my mind here so I'd help you out if I could, but I can't. I can't risk having anything delivered without having people know where I am."

"Couldn't you give me a number to call? Your name wouldn't have to be mentioned."

"I'm sorry," he laughs, "but it's too risky for me to help you out here. You'll have to find another way to get back at him," he says.

A rotund man with thinning hair walks into the bar and surveys the area as he bounces a set of keys in the palm of his hand. Noticing me, he walks over and asks, "You order a taxi?"

"Sure," I nod, "I'm Reverend Doyle."

"Well," the man says, "here I am."

Jack looks to him and asks, "Can we bring our beers?"

"Sure," the driver replies. "Just be sure not to spill them in the back."

"Can we smoke in the back?"

"I'm afraid not," he says, "rules are rules."

"Rules are rules," I say right back to him and I lift the nearest beer-mat from the table before rising to my feet.

"Souvenir?" Jack laughs.

"Hole in my shoe," I tell him.

31

THE BATHWATER ISN'T as hot as I'd like it to be but I'm too comfortable to sit up and lean over to the hot water tap near my feet. The beard I've grown is thick and unkempt, the water I'm in doing little to straighten out the bundled knots of hair. But water and the rising steam combined make the smell on my beard, the smell of Maria Leeson's pussy, almost impossible to ignore. That's the trouble with having even a little facial hair and soaking in the bathtub if you've just pleased a girl with your tongue; you smell her gash clearer than you did when you were down there.

Maria is fast asleep in the next room. Asleep in the next room where, not too long ago, she had claimed she could taste herself on my lips and chin.

Say what you will about pretty girls... About how they only lead to trouble or make graves, they just don't have the stamina. If you bring them to more than one orgasm, they're out for the count while you're still pulling a soiled rubber from your member. They're out for the count and even a major earthquake won't shake them back out of it.

The bathroom door opens and Laura Leeson walks into the room. She catches sight of me and is understandably horrified. "What are you doing here?" she screams.

"It's not how it looks," is all I can think of saying to her.

"Jesus!" She cries, "Jesus!" and then she storms out of the bathroom with intentions of calling the law. I jump out of the bathtub with hopes of somehow managing to talk her out of it and I take the towel from the radiator and try to wrap it around my waist but it's too small and my ass is left on display. I try to run after her anyway, racing down the narrow staircase I'm guessing she ran down and into the living-room where I notice a barn owl on display in a cage. The bird looks so old, so fragile, that I have to stop and look at it. It's funny but just looking at the bird leaves me with a feeling of love growing deep inside of me.

I wake up with the dream still on my mind and wipe a tear from my eye… Maybe it's something to do with the dream, maybe it's not. But I'm on Jack's bed in room four of the Four Card and it's late and the electric light is on and so is his iPod. The iPod is playing music so loudly that I can't imagine how I ever managed to fall asleep to begin with until I notice the acrid smell of marijuana in the air.

I sit up and the room spins around me. The sudden movement has blood pounding at my temple and I groan, rub my eyes and can't see Jack for a second or two. The top half of his body is in the bathroom, curled around the toilet, whereas his legs are sprawled into this part of the room. He's clearly out for the count. Maybe he's even vomited, maybe he hasn't. You can't smell it for the overpowering smell of cigarette smoke and marijuana.

I groan and manage to pull myself to my feet. The room starts spinning around me all over again and I consider turning the music off in case anybody complains about it, but I feel like shit so I'm feeling at my most selfish and I stumble for the door instead, deciding Jack can deal with whatever complaints might be thrown at him. I stop at the door, pat myself down for my keys and take one last look back to be sure I haven't forgotten anything before stepping outside and into the chilly air and darkness of early morning. I've barely closed the door behind me before I double over and barf all over the sidewalk. I barf again and notice how hot it is, like I'm bringing up boiling water.

"Jesus," I mutter, bringing my head up, smiling as I wonder if Mitch is watching all of this. But the smile is short lived and I barf for a third and final time. Even though I know the door to Jack's room is unlocked, I consider sleeping outside just so I won't have to move any more. I consider it long and hard but eventually I pull myself to my feet, leaning on Jack's 4X4 for support and drag my sorry ass towards my own room. For a reason I can't explain other than to try and amuse myself, I attempt to yank one of the wing-mirrors from Jack's ride but only succeed in knocking it askew. "Fuck it," I say with a sigh, taking the key from my pocket and slipping it into the lock of door number three.

32

I WAKE UP in my bed at the Four Card and realise that as well as feeling like shit, I'm still drunk and that doesn't seem fair. I should feel like shit or I should still be drunk but I certainly shouldn't be experiencing them both. I groan, try and remember what I was just dreaming about but fail. I want to fall back to sleep but can't because I feel so bad.. It feels like all the blood in my body is rushing to my head and refusing to move back down. And then I hear the scratching sound and wonder how I have only just noticed it. It's coming from outside and every time I think I've noticed a rhythm to the sound, a new one takes its place. It's the changing of the rhythm that makes it hard to ignore it all… Makes it so irritating.

"What the fuck is that?" I mutter, slowly pulling myself to my feet whilst lighting a cigarette. I cough a little and rush to the bathroom just in case I'm about to barf but I don't. I gather my breathing along with my thoughts before walking over to the door. The scratching appears a hell of a lot louder. I unlock the door as quietly as I can, certain that whatever is making the noise will rush into hiding if it knows I'm coming to investigate.

I finally step outside to investigate. Mitch is responsible for the noise; he's on his hands and knees with a brush in his hand and a bucket of soapy water to his side. The ground around him is soaking wet and covered in soapsuds. After a moment or two I remember how I hurled coming back to my room and when Mitch raises his head to look at me with anger in his eyes, I wonder what the chances really are of him having seen me do it.

"You seen this?" he snaps, never once stopping his hand from moving the brush across the ground.

"No," I answer weakly and swallow. "What is it," I ask, "kids with chalk?"

"I wish," Mitch says, shaking his head. "Vomit was all over the floor here," he says, raising his voice as if he wants Jack to hear.

"And do you smell that?" he asks me, still using his *loud voice*. "I could swear somebody here has been smoking a little Mary Jane."

"Mary Jane?" I ask like an innocent would.

"Marijuana," Mitch explains. "Dope. Grass. There's a damn bathroom in every room," he hisses on looking back to the wet ground beneath him, "so why you'd have to run out here to barf is anybody's guess."

"You know," I tell him, "just because somebody has been sick outside your motel, it doesn't mean they're staying at the motel. It could have been kids coming back from their first party or something."

"No," Mitch says as he shakes his head from side to side. "You stand where I'm at right now and you can smell the shit he was smoking. I'd bet the inside of room four smells a lot worse."

"You tried talking with him about it?" I ask out of interest.

"Sure have," Mitch says and he takes to scrubbing a little harder at one patch like he's determined to remove a stain only he can see. "Got no answer. I was going to let myself in but I thought it best to clear up first... before too many people see the state of the place. But I'll knock again a little later," he says. "If the man thinks he isn't getting charged extra for what he's got me doing here, he's got another thing coming."

"Sure," I say, feeling more than a little guilty, "I bet he has." I continue watching Mitch for a while before tossing the end of my cigarette into the middle of the road, as far from the patch he's working on as I can manage. "I'm going back inside," I tell him.

"Okay," he replies without looking up from the *new* patch he's now focusing all of his attention on, "don't let my attitude ruin your day."

I step back into my room and take to smirking as soon as the door is closed. It's an embarrassed kind of smiling I'm doing because I'm wondering if maybe I should have stepped up for Jack and said I'd gone out for something to eat and took to throwing up on the way home. The only problem with doing that would be Mitch wanting to know exactly where I'd been eating and soon everybody in town would be blaming some unfortunate diner the moment somebody even happened to sneeze.

"Better to stay quiet," I sigh in a desperate attempt to make myself feel a little better. It doesn't work so I light another cigarette and head into the bathroom with thoughts of taking a quick shower. I only catch the briefest of glimpses of my reflection in the mirror but it's more than enough to have me stop and take a better look. Something just doesn't sit right, so I stare long and hard at myself to try and work out just what it is and once I realise the answer I can't help but take a sharp intake of breath.

The off-white collar is no longer at my throat.

I take a step back and look to the floor but can't find sight of it. I rush into the bedroom and start pulling covers aside but it refuses to be found.

"Fuck," I mutter under the sound of my rapidly beating heart. "Fuck," I repeat, trying to remember when I was last wearing it. I'm sure I was wearing it when I returned here last night but I could be wrong. It could maybe be in Jack's room, or it could be heavy with the weight of vomit and soapy water it has been forced to absorb. If that's how it is, there's a chance Mitch will soon realise just what it is he has found.

I race to the window as quietly as I can manage and discreetly pull a section of curtain back to take a look. He's still on his hands and knees, still scrubbing away. If he has found my identity, dripping with bile and poison as its bitter stench floods his nostrils, he's yet to realise. And I realise how I am too tired to carry on caring. Smiling to myself, I make my way back to the bed and close my eyes. Just to make myself that little bit more comfortable, I take off my shirt and toss it towards the bathroom.

33

I**T'S REAL COLD** when I wake up. It's real cold and real dark… impossible to even see the nose in front of your face.

I spend what could be an hour but is probably a lot longer just sitting up on the bed, rubbing my left thumb back and forth over the nearest finger while I think things over. I think about what Jack had told me and wonder if he exaggerated events or kept parts from me. He's come a long way just to hide from a kicking and some stern words. I wonder if maybe his life could be in danger but he just doesn't want to admit to it yet.

And he could have made it all up but I don't mind. Everybody is a bullshitter but not everybody will buy your drinks.

And I think about Leeson and wonder if he's thinking about me right now. Has he figured out who I am yet and, even if he has, does it matter? I go on moving my thumb along the side of my finger and I try to think of new ways to go about hurting him. I try to think of a way that will have me knowing I destroyed some of the good inside of him. And Leeson will know it, too, and that's just something you can never forget.

Somebody knocks at the door. I stop moving my thumb over my finger and stop breathing for a second or so, just keeping my eyes on the door I can barely see for the darkness of the room, and then I turn on the bedside lamp and jump off the bed. I open the door without putting a shirt on first and see Maria Leeson waiting outside. She smiles a real nervous smile- I'm betting I'm the first guy she has ever seen going shirtless without being in a movie or fashion magazine, but invites herself in regardless. She deserves a round of applause for that but I notice Jack's 4X4 isn't parked outside and I find myself being distracted. "Shit," I say stepping into the cold night air. I bury my hands deep inside my trouser pockets, like I'm only cold because my hands are exposed and look up and down the street but the 4X4 is nowhere to be seen. "Shit," I say again.

"What is it?" Maria asks from behind me, reminding me of why I had opened the door in the first place. "What's wrong?"

"It's nothing," I say, shaking my head, stepping back inside the room and closing the door shut. Maria is standing to the side of the bed. I notice how she's wearing a little makeup; maybe even a little perfume. "It looks like the guy from the next room has been moved on or decided it was time to go."

"Were you two friends?"

"I don't know," I shrug, "maybe. Anyway," I say, "take a seat."

Maria looks to the bed, to me, to the bed again and then sits on the very edge of the mattress. I'm serious, the majority of her young ass is probably hovering in the air. I decide it best to wait a little while before sitting next to her, just in case she panics and falls to the floor so I sit on the floor beside the TV and reach into my pockets for my cigarettes but have no luck in finding any. "Shit," I mutter.

Maria says, "Something wrong?"

"A little," I sigh. "I can't find my cigarettes."

Maria reaches into one of her pockets and slips out a packet of Millbrooks and a disposable lighter. I bet the cigarettes were lifted from her mother's private stash. Her mother will also be looking all over the kitchen for her lighter when it's time to start cooking the next meal. "You want one?" she asks; trying her best to appear all grown-up as she places one between her soft lips and holds the open pack out for me to help myself.

"You're an angel," I smile at her, taking a smoke for myself. Maria lights her cigarette before handing me the lighter. I light up, pass it back to her. "How long have you been smoking?"

"I don't know," she says with a shrug, all cool, "a year, maybe a little longer."

I watch her take another drag and how she opens her mouth wide open right after, allowing the smoke to twist and curl before it floats back out into the open. At a guess, I'd say she's smoking very much like President Clinton claimed he did marijuana whilst at college- e.g. not inhaling. But I don't bring it up because I don't want the sweet little thing to feel uncomfortable.

I nod my head as if in understanding and pull cold yet heavy smoke into my lungs. "You really should try and quit while you're still young," I tell her. "It gets harder to quit the older you get."

"I've heard that," she says and I notice how every time she takes a drag on her cigarette, the two fingers she keeps it between move away from one another and it reminds me of a gal opening her legs so her man can slip his piece deep inside of her that little bit easier. "It's just that there's nothing to do in this town."

"I know it's hard," I tell her, "growing up in a town like this, but smoking isn't the answer. Even if it doesn't blacken your lungs," I warn, "it'll age the skin. Girl like you…" I say, "look at you. Why'd you want to ruin the natural beauty God went and gave you?"

She blushes but I act like I don't notice. I get the feeling she wants to say something, is desperate to say something, but is struggling to. I stay quiet, hoping she'll finally open her mouth and say it already. At long last, she does. "I thought you were going to get some alcohol in for when I came to visit?" she says as if to remind me.

I smile at her and slowly blow the cigarette smoke from my mouth. "Sure," I say once it's all gone, "I remember saying that, but I've had to pay an unexpected bill or two. But I'll tell you what," I add all generous like, "you slip me a twenty now and I'll get us a bottle or something."

There's disappointment behind her eyes on finding out she's expected to buy the alcohol but what can I say? Well, it takes all of my self control not to laugh and say, "Welcome to the twenty-first century; this is exactly how things are done now!"

And she's a twenty-first century girl. I remember, telling Cole as we were standing beside Tiffany Lily's pool, how all girls destined to become women this century are happy to do anal. Standing here now, I can't help but hope that was a statement of truth and not just a conversational piece. Maria throws me a smile anyway, like it's not a big deal, and reaches for her purse at the bottom of her bag. "Sure," she says, lifting two tens from plastic with a leopard-print decoration. She holds the two bills between two fingers and I playfully snatch them from her.

"What's your poison?" I ask.

There's a knock at the door and you can see the girl's heart must have frozen just by looking at her face, like she's terrified her daddy followed her over here. I offer her a reassuring smile and say, "Hold on a minute," before turning to see who else has come over for a visit tonight.

"Should I go hide in the bathroom?" she asks from my back.

"No," I chuckle, unlocking the door, "it'll probably be the guy from next door."

Turns out it isn't the guy from next door, it's Mitch. He's standing outside like he's spotted smoke creeping out from under my door and first he just throws me this real look of surprise- what with my wearing no shirt, and then he stands on the tips of his toes to get a look behind me, making sure it was Maria Leeson he saw coming in here. "Reverend Doyle," he says and it seems that's all he's capable of saying at the minute... That's all he's had time to think of saying.

"Mitch," I say back to him. "What can I do you for?"

He drops to the flat of his feet, glances at me and then tries to look over my shoulder for a second time. "That Maria Leeson you got in there with you?"

"Yes," I say, "it's the reverend's daughter." I step aside like I'm welcoming him on in and he sees her hovering over the very edge of the bed, real nervous. "I forgot she was calling by," I smirk at him, "so I forgot to get ready. But I'm about to throw a shirt on and then she's taking me out to see a couple of things before I take her back home."

"Oh," he says, "Oh."

You know what I've said doesn't sit right with him but he isn't sure what he should do now. "It's a little late," he says to me, "isn't it?"

"Girl's had school all day," I explain with a warm smile, "then she's had to do her homework before having her dinner." I look back to her, notice the cigarette she was holding looks to have magically disappeared and say, "but we won't be too long now, will we?"

"No," she says with a shake of her head, "Reverend Doyle."

"Oh," he says again, his eyes stuck to her this time. "Do your parents know you're here?"

"It was their idea," she replies.

"Oh," he says and he takes a retreating step before taking a look at me whilst inhaling deeply. "So where is it you two are going?" he needs to know.

"I'm the stranger in town," I smirk, "how should I know? But anyway," I sigh, "it's a little chilly and I promised to have her back home before it gets too late."

"Sure," he says, taking a couple more steps back to his office, "you two have a good night. Let me know if there's anything you need when you get back after seeing her home," he adds reluctantly turning his back to me.

"I will," I say and then I cheerfully shut the door and clamp a hand over my mouth to stop myself from laughing.

"Shit," Maria says, jumping to her feet, "shit," she says again as she pulls the covers back to reveal where she hid the cigarette. A hole has been made on the other side of the blanket, the area around it blackened by the heat. She takes the flattened but still smoking cigarette and drops it onto the carpet before stepping down on it. "What're we going to do now?" she asks me, her eyes wide with panic.

"Easy," I say to her with a smile, stepping closer and tenderly placing my hands atop of her shoulders. "We can still have a drink; just not here or too much, because we can't have you going home drunk now, can we?"

She releases a heavy-sounding sigh and says, "I'm sorry."

"What have you got to be sorry about?" I ask before planting a kiss upon her smooth forehead. "Now give me a minute to get ready and we'll be out of here," I confidently say to her. "Make a point of waving at his window when we're leaving," I smirk, "even if you can't see him standing there."

34

WE DON'T SPOT Mitch watching us as we leave but I've a feeling he is anyway and I wonder if he'll pick up the telephone and call Leeson right away or whether he'll wait to see if I try to bring Maria back with me. Maria looks to have lost the nerves she displayed hearing somebody knock on the door but she keeps giggling and it's hard for me to tell whether she's giggling with excitement caused by being with me or whether the giggling is down to her worrying about Mitch calling her old man. "You look different," she finally says.

"Really?" I ask her, "How so?"

We turn off Central Street and head down a road which is just as quiet, like everybody respectable in Whicker keeps themselves out of sight after dark or something. "I don't know," she smirks, "you just do." We carry on walking and after a little while, she claps her hands together and joyfully announces, "I've got it! It's the collar," she says, "you look so different without the white collar!"

"How about that?" I smile at her. "Who'd have thought something like that could make such a difference?" And I find myself thinking of Doyle even though I wish I wasn't, because it makes me feel a little sad and I have to keep it hidden from Maria. I wonder if Doyle is watching me from Heaven and what he must think about my behaviour right now if he is. Even the brightest stars in the sky remind me of Doyle from time to time, because he once told me how he'd read we all contain something of the stars in our DNA from when comets or meteors or whatever crashed into the Earth millions upon millions of years ago. That's how we'd live on forever more in the heavens, he once said. Because the light keeps burning long after the stars are gone. They continue to shine so long, you may as well count it as an eternity.

"Where is it?" Maria asks, and the sound of her angelic voice pulls me back from my own, personal thoughts.

"The dog collar?"

"Yes," she wants to know, "where is it? Are you not wearing it because people in town have an idea to who you are now or are you trying to go about Whicker *incognito*?"

"It's nothing so exciting," I laugh. "I misplaced it."

"You misplaced it?"

"Okay," I smirk, "okay, I *lost* it. Are you happy now?"

"Very," she says, and she playfully slaps my elbow. "I could get you another," she says after a moment. "If you feel you need one, that is."

I tell her, "That would be real kind of you if you could. Would you have to order it online or something? I'm only asking because I won't be in town that much longer."

"Nah," she says, "I won't have to do anything like that; I'll just take one from my dad's drawer, he has a lot of them. That won't be anything offensive, will it? I mean," she asks, "you both have the right to wear them, right?"

"Right," I say to her with a smile. "But just don't tell your mom or dad about it. They might not like the idea of us hanging out like this."

"I won't," she blushes, needlessly pushing a little hair behind her ear. "But you're moving on soon?"

"Sure am," I sigh. "Plan was always to spend just a week or so here."

"That's too bad," she says with a smile, "and there will be me, always wondering what I could have done to make you stay."

"Don't yank at my chain like that," I laugh, "you know I've got to go… People could start asking too many questions about me if I were to stay."

"I know," she says, "I know. But if you get the job in the town near here," she says, "maybe you could come by from time to time, or I could go visit you?"

"Sure," I say, "that could be fun," and Maria smile, hearing that, blushes again and lowers her head. "Where is it you're taking me to right now, anyway?"

"I don't know," she laughs, "I just like it being the two of us."

"Yeah," I smile at her, "so do I. But we're going to have to find somewhere… We can't go on walking the streets like this." I remember the twenty dollars she handed me back at the motel and the couple of bills I have to myself and ask her, "How about a bar? Is there someplace near here we could get a drink?"

"I don't think so," she says, clearly a little embarrassed. "They'll all know I'm under twenty-one and ask for ID seeing how I'm the reverend's daughter."

"How about a store where we could buy a little something to drink? We could take it to the park or something," I suggest, "and then I'll walk you back home."

"That'd be great," Maria says, "there's a place not too far from here that'll still be open."

The store turns out to be a little farther than I had assumed it would be, right by the place where Sam Pennington works. Maria waits outside - well, hidden around the corner - while I go on in and buy a cheap bottle of wine, a pack of paper cups (we can take two out and toss the rest in the trash), a ten-pack of Marlboros and some spearmint chewing gum so Maria can at least try and hide the smell of cigarettes and alcohol on her breath when she returns home. "What'd you get?" she asks the moment we regroup, eyes moving over the contents of the bag.

"Cheap but reasonably strong wine, a pack of smokes and some gum."

"Party cups?" she laughs. "Whose birthday is it?"

"We can pretend it's yours."

"Sure," she says, "how old would you like me to be?"

35

Don't ask me to explain *how*, but I've travelled back in time. My mind and every bit of knowledge it possesses has come to be in control of my body when it was only seven years of age. I'm fully aware I could have taken over myself at any age, at any moment, and I have opted for a bright yet meaningless day. I could have visited my grandmother on her deathbed and offered her words of comfort. I could have begged my brother not to leave me. I could have turned to Uncle Nick and tried to make him see how wrong his behaviour was. I could have even gone to see Doyle and talked him out of robbing Liefeld and Sons just one last time. Instead, I'm in the backyard (only our property was never so well kept) and I'm simply watching the pet cat (we never had a cat), Stronty, as he creeps alongside the tall bushes, stalking something unseen.

Stronty leaps into the bushes and quickly jumps back out of them with a large, black rat in his jaws. He shakes the rat, breaking its neck. Proud of his kill, he sinks the claws of a front paw into the body and separates the head from the neck, the rodent's skin stretching like black plastic, before devouring all of the remains. Stronty takes to walking alongside the bushes again, is soon stalking an unknown creature, and dives back out of sight, only to return with yet another rat to eat and kill in his favoured manner.

All of sudden, I'm standing in dad's shed… the shed he never had, and it's filled with cages holding numerous kinds of birds but they're mostly budgerigars. I'm delicately holding an injured pigeon in my two hands and I carefully place it inside an empty cage with intentions of leaving it to recover. I take one last look at the bird, hoping a rat won't somehow get a hold of it, and step out of the shed to get some birdseed from the kitchen cupboard. But I don't make it back to the house because my brother is waiting for me right outside the shed. He's around sixteen years old, just like he was when he left me, and he's angry. He violently lifts me by the throat and pulls a clenched fist back with thoughts of beating me but I'm not scared. I'm not scared because I'm a lot older than him despite my appearance, so I'm sure I can take him.

But he doesn't punch me. A look of realisation sweeps over his face and his fist trembles before he finally lowers it. "Doyle," he says.

"Leeson," I say back to him.

I wake up in my room at the motel and spend the most fleeting of moments trying to work out what the dream could have meant. Then I sit up and smile on remembering what I got up to last night. My lips seem to tingle as I remember kissing Maria in the park, the bitter taste of cheap wine on her plump lips. I'd love to say I was her first kiss but I doubt it, what with the way she looks. But she clearly hasn't kissed too many boys because her technique is pretty bad. She had insisted on forcing her tongue as far into my mouth as she possibly could and that was basically all. But was I the first guy to cop a feel of her firm tits? Well, here's hoping…

I'd walked her most of the way home, the two of us stopping a few doors down from her place to try and avoid being seen by her parents or anybody else. Or so she had believed. When I had kissed her goodbye, I'd been wishing for a neighbour to spot us. That's why I had kissed her for so long and so passionately. After finally saying our goodbyes, I had returned back here to enjoy one last cigarette before jacking-off and calling it a night. All in all, it had been a real fine night for me.

Still smiling, I get out of bed and pull on my trousers before heading over to the window. I don't have to move the net curtain aside to see Jack's 4X4 is back outside and I'm relieved to see it. Coming back here late last night to see it was still missing, I'd been sure Mitch had moved him on and I'd have nobody to discuss my seduction of Maria Leeson with. But Jack is next door and so I'll soon be telling him all about it.

I shower, dress and step out of my room with thoughts of calling for Jack but Mitch is standing outside his own door, clearly waiting for me. "Reverend Doyle," he calls out to me.

"Good morning."

"Right," he says. "I'd like to have a word with you."

"That won't be a problem," I tell him. "I've just got some business to take care of and then-"

"Now," he insists, turning back to his room/office, knowing full well I'll follow him. Trying not to smile with excitement, I make my way into room number one. It's the exact same size as the other rooms I've seen but there's no bed, no TV; just a leather chair on either side of a glass table and a collection of numbered keys hanging on the wall. Mitch is already sitting in one chair, facing me. I notice the stainless steel flask underneath his chair but don't mention it. "Close the door," he sighs. "Take a seat."

Filled with curiosity, I do exactly what is asked of me. It takes him a moment or two to figure out just what it is he wants to say, so I light up a cigarette without first asking if that would be okay or whether he would care to join me. But I'm more than sure he wouldn't care to join me at this moment or any other moment that should follow.

"You've been here the best part of a week," he says.

"I sure have," I say and I know I'm interrupting. "If you're wondering how I'm finding my stay," I smile at him, "I couldn't ask for a better place or better people."

He looks away, scratches the side of his neck and then looks back at me. "Reverend Doyle," he says, "I called you here to tell you I think it's time you moved on."

36

THE TWO OF us just sit there, looking at one another in silence. It's so silent that when I take a drag on my cigarette, you hear the soft crackling of burning tobacco or cigarette paper or both. "Is that so?" I finally ask him, "What makes you say that?"

Mitch takes a deep breath and sighs before pretending to pluck something that isn't there from his trouser leg. "I made a mistake," he says without looking at me. "I can't afford to give you the room for the price you're having it."

"What if I can pay the full rate?" I smirk.

"It's not just that," he claims. "There's going to be a big business conference of some kind in the next couple of days, and I clean forgot about it. You see," he says, "the big hotel is already fully booked and I promised a couple of people attending the conference that they could stay here. Told them a while ago," he says, "which is why I forgot. But I found the records earlier today and thought it best I tell you about it sooner rather than later."

"Sure," I nod. "You say they're coming in the next couple of days, so I'll leave when they arrive. It'll suit all of us just fine."

"I'm sorry," he says, "and I'd let you stay on until then if I could, but they're arriving a day or two *before* the conference. You know how it is," he shrugs. "They want to have a day or so looking around the town before getting down to business."

I nod my head and drop a little ash onto the floor beside me. "May I see them?"

Mitch looks to me and asks, "See *what*?"

"These records of yours," I reply. "May I see them?"

Mitch takes another deep breath before responding, the inhaling there just to buy him a little extra time. "I'm afraid not," he says. "Confidentiality agreements and the like."

"I'm a man of God," I smile, "I'm sure they won't mind."

"Well," he says as if it pains him to do so, "it's not like I can ask them whether they would or not if they're not here, is it?"

I nod again, smile and drop a little more ash onto the floor before taking another drag on my cigarette. "I see," I tell him, "I see. You know something," I grin, "I don't believe a single word that's coming out of your mouth."

"Oh?"

"Nope," I say, "not a word."

"Well," he says, puffing out his chest, "I don't think that matters because I'm in charge of the Four Card."

"You are," I nod, "and you want me out of here because of my friendship with Maria Leeson, don't you?"

"I don't-"

"You know full well what I'm talking about, Mitch. It's that simple, you aren't happy about me spending time with Maria. I understand why you'd want to look out for her... for him... After all," I smile, "I hear you were a desperate coke addict before he stepped in."

"How do you-"

"He *told* me," I smile. "He told me just how pathetic he found you and your problems... just like he finds the problems of every fucker in this worthless town."

"No," he says, shaking his head from side to side. "I don't believe you. Not one bit. Paul isn't like that."

"Then believe *this*," I advise, leaning forward in my chair, "your moving me out of here when I'm not ready to go without a good cause would see the people around town talking. And you know what could happen while they're talking in hushed voices? The Leeson family could take me in," I smile at him, "because it would be the charitable thing to do."

"No," he says, "I wouldn't let them."

"You'd have to give them a reason," I shrug. "You going to tell people you caught Maria Leeson in my room last night and I was close to being undressed? You won't tell them that," I say, "and it's not just because you're scared the story will make its way all over town; you're scared of hurting the family. Be honest," I laugh, "you considered calling the law, didn't you? You didn't because you're desperate for nobody else to find out about your suspicions. People will be talking all about sweet, young Maria. And what if she's sweet on me?" I smile at him, take another drag on my cigarette. "What a romantic tragedy it could be," I tell him, "my being taken away in the back of a police car. But that would be after a long trial," I grin, "and that would only be if you're right. And what if you're wrong? It doesn't matter," I say with another nonchalant shrug of my shoulders, "because everybody in town will have already been talking about it by then. The damage would have been done. The girl will never be looked at in the same way again, not by the good people of Whicker, anyway."

Mitch takes a cheap-looking cigar from one of his pockets and tears the cellophane from it with his clumsy, trembling fingers. I wait in silence as he lights up before looking over the dancing flame to ask me, "Why are you doing this?"

I smirk, shrug my shoulders and lean closer to the table so I can stub my cigarette out on it. "I'm not doing anything," I tell him. "There is nothing happening outside that perverted little mind of yours. I'm a respectable man of God while you're," I say, "you're a recovering drug addict running a rundown motel."

And with that, I get to my feet and walk out of room number one. I'm a little surprised to see Sam Pennington pacing up and down, looking to each and every door from number two onwards without knowing where exactly to stop, her rusting Beetle parked nearby. I clear my throat and say, "Sam?"

It's impossible not to see the look of relief on her face the second she catches sight of me. "Reverend Doyle," she says, "thank God I found you."

37

SEEING HOW I can't really invite Sam into my room for a coffee I suggest she drive us to any place nearby where we can buy one and she agrees. As we're driving away from the Four Card, I spot Mitch watching us from the doorway of room one but think nothing of it. I'm too interested in Sam. I know she hasn't tracked me down because she's looking for an easy lay but I'd sure like to know what has got her so close to tears.

We get out of the car soon enough and make our way to a table inside a cosy diner. She takes a moment to compose herself once our drinks have arrived and then she begins. "It's Danny," she says, shaking her head from side to side as she tries to make sense of it all and leaves me desperately hanging. "He's… *playing-up*," she says, using an expression I haven't heard for years as if that explains it all and in return I offer her the nearest thing to a warm, caring smile that I can give.

I want to know, "How so?"

Sam sighs and shakes her head from side to side once again; wraps both hands around her cup and pulls it toward her. "I haven't even been able to go into work," she says, the master storyteller leaving me in suspense for as long as possible whenever she can. "I didn't like the idea of leaving him in the house for too long. I didn't know what to do but then I remembered you."

"You did the right thing," I assure her. "Now," I ask, "just tell me what the problem is and I'll see what we can do about it."

She shakes her head from side to side yet again and wipes a tear from her eye. It's seeing the tear that has me feeling more than a little sorry for her. "It would be an understatement," she says, "if I told you his attitude, his behaviour, has gone from bad to worse. A *huge* understatement," she says. "It's like he's gone away and been replaced by somebody that looks like him… Somebody nasty. He's pretty much taken control of the house," she says, her voice starting to break.

"Take it easy," I say. "Try not to even think about it. Let's enjoy our coffees and then you can take me back to your place and I'll nip this in the bud once and for all."

"I'm sorry," she laughs, "but I don't think he'll listen, not to you and certainly not to me. I just had to tell somebody," she says.

"I'm still going to give it my best."

I drink my coffee slowly to give her time to catch up but she doesn't even touch hers; she just stares at it and keeps whatever thoughts she's having to herself. I stand up and suggest we head over to her place and she offers no resistance, we just climb back inside her car that shakes and sticks between gears and drive over to her home with the radio on to cover an uncomfortable silence. The local station is playing Bon Iver when we come to stopping outside her place and we both look to it without offering a single word. It looks as homely as it did the last time I was here.

"Is Danny in?"

"He was when I left," she says, still looking at the house. "I don't know if he had any plans to go someplace."

I nod my head whilst unfastening my seatbelt. "Is the door open?"

"I left it on the latch," she sighs, still looking over at the house. "If he's gone out," she says, "he's probably left it open anyway."

"Stay here," I tell her as I step out of the vehicle.

"You don't want me to come in with you?"

"No," I smile at her. "You just wait out here and let me try and talk with him alone. I'll be as quick as I can."

"Okay," she says right as I slam the car door shut. I walk straight to the house and try to decide whether I can hear music or not as I get closer to it. When I push the front door open, I know for sure it was music I could hear, or something pretending to be music. It's all distorted guitars and a throbbing bass to drums and somebody singing in a way that's probably going to leave him with polyps. And then there's the bitter smell of pot. I know Danny is in his bedroom in the way you can enter a place and just know you're not the only one there. I smile to myself and turn to slowly close the door behind me and Sam, still looking to the house from her place in the car, thinks the smile is meant for her and smiles back in my direction.

I close the door and softly chuckle to myself.

38

I RECOGNISE THE music as Marilyn Manson, a shock-rocker who shocks next to nobody these days regardless of how desperate he can be. But this is a small town and because of that, young Danny Pennington probably thinks old Marilyn is simply the bees-knees for pissing off the establishment.

I wonder if Danny Pennington has ever wandered into a record store and asked *why* they insist on selling vinyl records...

The track finishes and in the short silence before the next one begins, I have all the time I need to bring my thoughts back to the here and now. I smile and, not wanting to be unexpectedly disturbed if I can prevent it, I lock the door before heading on into the kitchen. I pour myself a glass of chilled orange juice and lean against a worktop. Enjoying a cigarette, I can hear Danny moving about upstairs. He's making about as much noise as an elephant.

A part of me hopes he'll come rushing down the stairs and find me waiting here for him but it doesn't happen. I finish my cigarette, down my drink and slowly make my up the stairs as quiet as a mouse. I see the poster for Rob Zombie's Halloween sequel before I'm even on the landing. It's no longer stuck to Danny's bedroom door but lies discarded on the floor. Every inch, from the very top to the very bottom of Danny's bedroom door is covered with pictures of the same two women. One is a brunette and the other is a redhead. Both are pretty (I'll admit I find one to be more attractive than the other) and both have their yams out and are a real pleasure to look at. I want to admire them a while longer, see if either or both of them has had any surgical enhancements, but I don't. I focus on the task at hand, see what I can gather.

At a guess, I'd say every single picture had been made available thanks to a home printer. Some pictures overlap onto others but some have been carefully sized before being printed- just to be sure no door space at all is left empty.

And that smell of burning marijuana has become so much stronger and all the more unpleasant. It's clearly pretty cheap grass he's smoking in the comfort of his room.

I ease the door open and get my first sight of him. For a second, he doesn't even know I'm there but that's more than enough time to weigh him up. Danny is pretty short and as scrawny as hell. I'm guessing his hair is pretty light in colour or he's lighting it before colouring it black, because it looks real thin on top like he's been dyeing it far too often. And he's sitting on his bed, flicking through a magazine called *Idols of Rage* (all block capitals) with a rock band on the cover I've never seen before. Danny in his black T-shirt and black jeans with a stainless steel chain running from beneath his shirt- curving into one of his trouser pockets and black sneakers with ridiculously high soles. He senses my presence, gives an uninterested glance in my direction but leaps to his feet and tosses the magazine aside, realising I'm not his downtrodden mother or friend of the family. He flinches like he was planning on rushing me but thought better of it at the last possible second. The attitude he's sporting is now that of a rabbit caught in the headlights. The difference not wearing an off-white dog collar makes is fucking astounding.

"Danny Pennington," I say.

"What do you want?" he croaks. The look in his eyes tells me he knows he sounded nowhere near as confident or as tough as he had hoped. The kid's probably longing to hear the sound of his mother returning home so can she save him. "Who the fuck are you?" he says, sounding a little braver this time.

"Do me a favour," I tell him, "and turn that bullshit off."

"Who the fuck are you?" he asks me for the second time.

"My name is Reverend Doyle," I reply and that's enough to make him smile, like I'm just some pussy he has no real cause to worry about. "Your mother thought it would be a good idea for the two of us to talk."

"Then talk," he says, flicking his shoulders forward.

"Then switch that bullshit off already."

"Bullshit," he smirks, walking a little out of sight but I step a little farther into the room and see the small device of black metal he's heading to. It's no bigger than a cellphone and I can't see any speakers attached to it so I have no idea how it can make such a racket but the music dies the second he presses a button. He turns back to face me, still smirking like the arrogant little shit that he is. "Well," he says, "what do you want?"

I try to make every step I take towards him as loud as it can be. "I want you to start showing your mother some respect," I tell him. "I want you to stop being such a little cunt and start going to school again."

"You can't talk to me like that," he snaps.

"I can," I say shoving him in the chest, "so I fucking do."

"Who the fuck-" he starts and he takes a step towards me but I shove him back before he can get as close as he would like to be.

"I've already told you my name," I calmly remind him. "And I've told you what I'm expecting from you. And Danny," I laugh, "there will be some serious fucking consequences if you think you can get away with not listening to me and pissing your mother off."

"You're not a reverend," he smirks. "You're a joke. You're a-" he snarls, moving his hand forward with intentions of pushing me in the face. But I take a tight hold of his wrist with one hand and wrap the other around his throat before spinning around to plant him on the floor. There's a split-second where he tries to figure out just what has happened and then he looks like he's ready to cry. Leaning over him to keep him down on the floor I look him right in the eye and speak softly, so he has to listen carefully. "You know those pictures you've got out on the landing?"

He tries to swallow and finds it a lot harder than it should be thanks to my grip on his throat. He opens his mouth but soon closes it and simply nods his head.

I ask him, "Who the fuck are they?"

"Just magazine girls," he says.

"Who the fuck *are* they?"

"I've told you already," he says, close to tears. "They're just girls from the magazines."

"Who… the… fuck… are… they?'

"What," he says, "you want their life story or something? One of them is called Zara Durose and the other is called Sophie Howard. I told you, they're just girls from the magazines… British girls," he desperately adds.

For a split-second I don't know what to say or do. It's just the way Danny said that they are *British girls*. It has me think of Uncle Nick with his skin-flicks from various parts of the world. A lot of the girls in those were British and now some youngster trying to convince us all he's dangerous shows an interest in girls from the same part of the world. I try to decide if there is a connection of some kind before realising it isn't important. I get back to the here and now.

"Well listen," I tell him, "Zara and Sophie are going to be long gone before your mother returns home. This room," I say, "is going to be real tidy. And your attitude," I smirk, "you're going to have a whole new one. Do you understand what I'm saying?"

"Who the fuck do you-"

I tighten my grip on his throat and he squeezes his eyes shut for a heartbeat. When he opens them, I'm guessing his vision is more than a little blurred for the tears. "Do you understand what I'm saying?"

"Yes," he croaks.

"That's good," I cheerfully announce, letting go of his wrist and his throat. "I'm glad we got this all sorted nice and easy. Don't let me find out you haven't taken me seriously."

A feeling of great pride takes control of me as I walk for the bedroom door, happy to know I've helped a troubled mother out in life. I'm about to take my first step onto the stairs when I hear clumsy footsteps rushing for me and I turn to see the little prick running at me with tears streaming down the mask of rage that his face has become. It's the flick-knife in his hand that really grabs my attention. The flick-knife with a chain leading from the handle, up to just beneath his shirt. Big old Danny sitting in his room with a knife in his pocket.

He opens his mouth to say something but I don't give him the chance. I slap him hard across the face with an open palm and the second he crashes into the wall, I throw a solid left into his stomach and he doubles over in pain. He's still struggling to breathe as I push him to the ground and keep him there by firmly planting a knee into his chest as I take the knife from his hand.

"You go to church, Danny?" I ask him and I don't know why but I'm panting like I'm out of breath. Danny's red as beetroot and struggling to draw enough air into his lungs. "Do you go to church, Danny- yes or no?" I ask on holding the blade just under his left eye.

"No," he gasps like a fish out of water.

"Shit," I say, "I haven't been paying much attention there myself," I tell him, moving the blade along to the other eye. "I can't remember which eye you remove if it offends you. Is it the right," I ask before moving the blade back to its original place, "or left?"

"Please," he whimpers.

"Are you going to do what I said?"

"Yes," he weeps.

"You promise?"

"Yes," he nods, shaking gently for the tears he can't hold back.

"You'd best not be yanking my chain," I warn him, "or I'll take something from you before you even get the chance to use it."

I snap the knife shut before dropping it and turn away from him, slowly making my way down the stairs. Sweat is prickling at my brow and I wipe it away using the back of my sleeve before reaching the front door and pulling the locks back out of place. "Hey," Danny calls out from the top of the stairs and I turn to see him standing there, looking down at me with disgust. "You think you can do that to me?"

"Danny," I smile, "I just did."

"Fuck you," he shouts and he points at me to say, "you don't know who I know."

"Jesus," I smirk, "everybody knows somebody these days."

"I tell them about this," he sneers, "and you're through. I mean it," he says, "you'll be fucked. You'll be a fucking ghost!"

"Danny," I say, pulling the door open, "as long as you're not involved and you're keeping in line, I really couldn't give a fuck."

39

Sam nervously asks as I'm fastening my seatbelt, "How did it go?"

"You mind if I have a cigarette?"

"Go right ahead," she says and as I'm lighting up she smiles weakly and adds, "that bad, huh?"

I blow smoke up toward the car ceiling. "He certainly has some attitude problems," I say, "but we sat down and had a little chat."

"He actually *talked* with you?" Sam asks in disbelief.

"Sure," I say with a nod. "He was a little arrogant at first but, you know something?"

"What?" she asks, eyes wider than I've ever seen them before.

"He had absolutely no idea how much his behaviour had been upsetting you," I tell her. "Not a clue. Danny was simply playing-up," I say, looking back to the house, "for attention." If he's watching us from behind one of the windows, I don't see him. If he's raiding his mom's cupboard for a gun she happens to keep hidden in case of an intruder, I have no idea how I'll react if he finds it and comes marching outside while we're still sitting here.

"I give him all the attention I can!" Sam exclaims. "He's the one who tries to make sure we're never in the same room together!"

"Well," I shrug, "he's an adolescent. Do you remember wanting to be around your parents so much when you were his age?"

"No," she laughs, "I mostly stayed in my room, listening to my records. But I never would have acted as bad as Danny has," she states, "I'd never have gotten away with that."

"And that's just it," I smile, "the boy needs discipline. He was pushing at you because he *wanted* you to bring him back under control. I know that might sound a little crazy-"

"No," she smiles, "it really doesn't."

I smile right back at her, drop my hand over of hers and give it a squeeze. "He's going to try harder," I tell her, "but you have to be able to reel him in whenever necessary."

"I will," she assures me, "I will. Thank you, Reverend Doyle. You don't know how much this means to me."

"It was nothing," I blush. "But anyway," I ask before she can pull me up on it, "what're you doing with the rest of your day? I only ask because I wouldn't go inside just yet," I smile, "because Danny is tidying his room with hopes of surprising you."

"You're kidding!"

"No," I say, "I'm really not. So if you'd like to drive me back to the Four Card-"

"Oh no," she says, starting the engine, "I can't let you just go back to your tiny room!" She grins at me and asks, "Would you like a drink, Reverend Doyle?"

"Call me Doyle," I tell her, wondering if this is how you get into her panties, disciplining her asshole son or appearing as something of a father-figure. "And sure," I say with a shrug, "a drink would be nice. But I should warn you," I joke only to remind her of the last time we drank together, "I haven't got my dancing-shoes on."

"Don't you worry about that," she laughs, moving the car forward, "we'll just go have a quick bite to eat and a drink to celebrate your good work. Seriously," she smiles to me, "you're a true miracle worker."

40

Sam happily brings the car to a stop outside Velma's and cheerfully announces, "Here we are."

"*This* is the place you wanted to get a bite to eat?" I ask. It's funny, it really is, because I've had so many different plans to try and hurt Leeson but I don't want to step into the bar, just in case the same member of staff I got talking to about Maria Leeson so recently is working again. I try to work out what my problem could be, whether I'm proud of how I've helped Sam out and I don't want it to be ruined by a young barman telling her something I've said or whether it's how I want to fuck Maria so I don't want to risk word of my drinking with Sam Pennington getting back to her and scuppering my chances.

And then maybe there could be some good inside of me, trying to break out... or am I simply trying to settle on the plan that could hurt Leeson the most?

I doubt it's the former, realising that if Sam and me have enough to drink, I'll only end up trying to worm my way into her bed and so I cast aside all thoughts of redeeming characteristics. I'm without those and without chance of redemption, because redemption can only be found through God.

"Well," Sam says with a smile, happy to believe all of her problems at home have been solved already, "I can only have the one because I'm driving, but I'll still buy us something to eat and you can have a couple of beers while I'm on the soda!"

I smile at her and shake my head from side to side. Knowing full well how I'll only end up hitting on her a little later (and maybe wanting to prove to myself I'm not turning into a pussy now everything is so close to coming together) I ask, "How did you ever get to be alone? I swear," I tell her, "you're my perfect woman."

"Ha," she blushes, "easy, Doyle, people will get the wrong idea now you're not wearing your collar." She reaches for a button to turn the radio off but I quickly move my hand forward so it lands on hers and she freezes because of it.

"You mind if we have a smoke before we go on in? If you don't," I say, as if to explain my most recent actions, "we may as well leave the radio on to have a little music."

Sam swallows and simply stares back at me for a moment. "Sure," she eventually smiles, "we can have a cigarette before going in."

We're lighting up when the local DJ finally stops talking and starts another song, but it's a One Direction track and it only has me wondering if it could be a sign how I would be better off spending my afternoon with Maria. "Boy," Sam says, blowing a faint trail of smoke from the corner of her mouth, eyes on the radio, "I really hate these guys. They're just so bland."

"Yeah," I nod in agreement, "the sooner these pricks disappear into obscurity, the better." Sam laughs at that. I laugh and ask her, "What's so funny?"

"You," she says, still laughing. "Are you sure you're a reverend?"

"I'm not at the minute," I smirk, "I can't find my dog collar."

"Misplacing your collar," she says, playfully shaking her head from side to side. "That's a clear sign you're a fake. But do you mind if I change stations," she says, moving her free hand towards another button on the radio, "or are you a secret One Direction fan, too?"

"Change the station," I chuckle, "I own all of their records, anyway."

Sam laughs at that and changes the station. The British boyband are immediately replaced by a news-report which we know will be followed by a song, so she sits back in her seat and takes a drag on her cigarette. "I can't remember the last time I felt this relaxed," Sam sighs.

"It's me and my soothing influence."

"It is," she grins in response, leaving me to wonder if we're flirting with one another or not right now. The news-report ends and a DJ comes back on the air to say nothing of interest for the best part of a minute and then a song begins- The Beach Boys' *I Know There's An Answer*. "Oh," Sam coos, "I love this song."

I nod my head in understanding. "Pet Sounds," I say. "It's a great record."

Sam asks, "You like The Beach Boys?"

"What I know of them," I reply. "My mom liked them. Not as much as The Beatles, but she used to play them from time to time."

"I've always preferred The Beach Boys. Who's your favourite?" she asks.

"Beach Boy? I don't know," I shrug, "I've never really been asked that before. But I guess I'll go with Brian, seeing as he was the key writer and producer."

"I always liked Dennis," Sam chuckles, "and it's not just because he was the hot one!"

I laugh, take a drag on my cigarette and blow the smoke out of my nostrils before talking again. "You know why they called the record *Pet Sounds*?"

"Yes," she says to me with a confident smile, like I should be ashamed for even daring to ask her that, "so the record had the same initials as Phil Spector."

"That's the popular story," I smile before adding, "I have a lot of time for Spector."

"He's crazy."

"No," I tell her, "he's just misunderstood. The man is a genius."

"A mad genius?"

"Okay," I laugh, "we'll agree to disagree on Spector and leave it at that." I look to my cigarette and see how it's almost finished and that can only mean we'll soon be heading into Velma's.

"How about the question you must have been asked before? Who is your favourite Beatle?"

"Ringo."

"Ringo?" Sam laughs. "Are you kidding?"

"No," I smirk, "he was a real nice guy. Why," I ask her, "who's yours?"

"George," she says without needing to give it a second's thought.

"Sure," I nod, "I can see why you would say that."

"So you were kidding," she smiles, "and George is really your favourite?"

"He's a close second," I claim and that only makes Sam laugh out loud.

She takes one last pull on her cigarette before opening her door to toss it out onto the asphalt. "Come on," she smiles, "I owe you lunch."

41

I HAVE A double-cheeseburger with chilli sauce, fries and a beer; Sam has the vegetarian lasagne with garlic mushrooms and a side of potato wedges she tells me to help myself to a Coca Cola. I have another couple of beers and Sam has a couple more cokes and then she orders herself dessert - double chocolate cheesecake - while I just have another beer. Then she orders herself a medium coffee and I have yet another beer. I'm already feeling a little merry by this point and being a little flirtatious but Sam doesn't seem to notice, or she simply *acts* like she doesn't notice and I wonder if getting sex would have meant telling her Danny was beyond hope.

"Well," Sam says to me as a barman comes over to collect the last plate, "I guess I should be heading back. Can I offer you a ride back to the Four Card?"

"No," I tell her, "I think I'll just have a couple more beers," I add, reaching a hand into my pocket, hoping she'll offer me a couple of bucks at least because I don't really want to spend what's left of my money.

"Don't be silly," she says, holding her hand out - the action causing me to immediately pause. "Ryan," she says to the barman who is still at our table, "make sure Reverend Doyle here gets whatever he'd like. Put it on my tab, would you?"

Ryan looks to me so he'll have an idea to who he shouldn't be charging and says, "Sure thing, Sam," before finally walking away.

I can't believe my good luck but I play at being embarrassed by the offer. "I really can't," I say.

"Of course you can," Sam insists with a smile. "I owe you a lot more," she adds but I don't read anything into that because of how my attempts at flirting went unnoticed, "but now I really should get going."

"I'll walk you out to your car."

"You don't have to do that."

"I insist," I say, rising from my chair, "I'll go outside for a quick smoke."

Sam waves goodbye to the workers as we head to the door and then we're back outside. The day is pretty bright but there's a chill to the air. I light a cigarette as we walk over to her car and ask, "You want one?"

"No," she says, "thank you," and I wonder if she hides her smoking from Danny, which would explain the electronic cigarette she smokes at home. If she does, it's probably more to stop him from stealing her smokes than it is caring about his health. And can you blame her? The boy's a total fucker.

"Here we are," I say as she unlocks the driver's door.

"Here we are," she repeats, turning to face me with a tender smile. Sam asks, "How much longer are you planning on staying in Whicker?"

"I don't know," I shrug, "a day or two." The decision is down to me wanting to be long gone before Sam next visits the bar and sees just how much of a bill I ran up once she had left me unsupervised.

"Come say goodbye before you leave," she says, wrapping her arms around me and planting a soft kiss upon my cheek but again, I read nothing into this. "You've done more than you know," she smiles and then she gets into her car and starts the engine. I take retreating steps back, waving as she reverses onto the road before turning to drive back home.

I finish my cigarette before heading back into Velma's for my first beer with a shot.

42

THE DRIVER TOSSES all rules and regulations right out of the window and allows me to light up in the back of his cab, immediately earning himself a decent tip I don't think I can even afford in doing so. I enjoy my cigarette and keep my eyes to the window so I can watch various areas of Whicker pass me by, the driver earning himself that little bit extra of a tip by not insisting we talk along the way.

And I feel good. The beers and the shots have me feeling as hard as nails and as tough as old boots. I know that I'm pretty drunk because I can feel it but I'm pretty sure the driver or anybody else won't notice it because of my self-control.

I try to figure out how much money I ended up placing on Sam Pennington's tab and chuckle, trying to imagine just how she'll react on finding out. The driver glances at me via the rear-view mirror, but only for the briefest of moments, like he was wondering if I was choking on something. I pretend I didn't notice.

We stop outside the church and I give him the fare with tip and say, "God bless you," with hopes he'll ask if I'm a reverend and refuse some of the money when I say that I am, but he doesn't ask me anything; he just thanks me and drives on down the road. "Asshole," I mutter under my breath, lighting another cigarette to enjoy before I head on into the church. The sun is starting to set but the doors to the church are still wide open, meaning Leeson is bound to be in there and I wonder how things could play out if Laura or Maria are in there with him.

I wonder if Mitch has spoken with him about recent events...

A sweet old lady comes walking out of the doors and smiles the moment she recognises me. She walks slowly and so I have plenty of time to remember where I know her from. I realise she was one of the two gals I sat with on first entering the church... one of the two who then stood out here with me until their ride turned up.

"Good evening," I smile to her once she's close enough.

"Good evening," she smiles. "I'm terribly sorry," she says, "but my memory isn't quite what it used to be and I can't remember your name!"

"Doyle," I tell her, "Reverend Doyle."

"That was it," she smiles with some relief and I try to remember whether I actually told her my name or not. I can't remember if she even told me hers, anyway. "Are you waiting for Reverend Leeson?" she asks.

"I'm just about to go in and have a quick chat with him," I cheerfully reply, "if he isn't too busy."

"Oh," she tells me, "he's never too busy. He always has time for people."

"Isn't that nice?" I ask her, "Is he in there on his own?"

"Yes," she says, glancing back at the church. "He just has a couple of things to look over and then he'll be done for the night."

"Let me guess," I smile, "he'll go let his hair down at the waffle place before heading home?"

She laughs at that. "Don't tell Laura," she says, "he always talks about eating right but whenever she's not looking, he's off eating something he shouldn't be!"

"Ha," I say, "that's definitely the Paul I know," before immediately adding, "I mean, Reverend Leeson." The old lady nods, comes to the decision that me and the good reverend must surely be friends of old. I wonder how long it will take for everybody in town to believe the same. Will they doubt him when he says he doesn't know me?

"It's going to be a warm night. The weather report keeps threatening us with rain, but I can't see that happening. Skies are as clear as crystal."

"They most certainly are," I agree, taking one last drag on my cigarette before flicking it out into the middle of the road. A car comes driving by and I hope it's whoever the old lady is waiting for but the vehicle goes on by without stopping and turns out of sight as soon as it can. "Are you waiting for somebody?" I ask.

"My neighbour said he would come and collect me," she says, still smiling. "You don't have to wait out here with me, you can go on in and speak with the reverend if you have to."

"No," I smile at her, "I'll keep you company."

"My," she laughs, "it's been a long time since I was seen talking with a handsome young man! And you without your collar," she says. "People will be talking about me all over town!"

"Go on and let them," I tell her, "it's only because they're jealous."

"Oh," she says once she stops laughing, "you're just as light-hearted as Reverend Leeson- maybe even more so. People must be missing you back home."

"I doubt it," I tell her and I light another cigarette before asking if she would care to join me.

"I'd best not," she grins, "the reverend will be very upset if he smells cigarette smoke on me tomorrow!"

"You're coming back here tomorrow?"

"I'm here most days of the week," she says with pride. "Tidying up, seeing appointments aren't forgotten about, just helping out in any way I can."

"It sounds to me like the townspeople should be coming to you for guidance."

"Oh," she laughs, "I don't know about that." A car comes towards us, gradually dropping its speed as the driver moves the vehicle closer to the kerb. "Well," she smiles, "it was a pleasure speaking with you again, Reverend Doyle."

"And you," I tell her as she climbs into the vehicle. The moment her seatbelt is fastened, the driver moves along and reluctantly waves to me alongside the cheery old lady. I wait until the car is out of sight before finishing my cigarette and making my way inside the church.

43

I FIND LEESON sitting at his desk in his private office or whatever, looking over notes or letters, and I'm surprised to see how he more or less sits with his back facing the door. Seriously, how easy must your life have been or how at ease must you be in your recent surroundings for you to have no problems or feelings of unease when it comes to sitting with your back to an open door? I know I could never do that, just as I know he doesn't sense my presence. I just stand there, watching him for a while, before turning and creeping back to the main place of worship. It stands deserted and so I make my way to a pew near the front and sit down with only my thoughts and a lifeless image of Christ for comfort.

After a while, I hear Leeson's footsteps as he leaves his office and takes to walking around his church, most likely checking everybody has gone home before locking up for the night. His footsteps come closer and closer, sound echoing around the confined corridors until they come to a sudden stop and he says, "Is there anything I can help you with?"

I smile, rise to my feet and turn around to face him. He's standing near the back of the church and it's easy to see how surprised he is at finding me on his turf. "Reverend Doyle," he says, "I didn't know that you were here. I'm sorry," he adds, "but I'm about to call it a day."

"No," I say, stepping into the aisle with a friendly grin, "you don't have to apologise for *that*." We're both standing at separate ends of the aisle now, facing one another like gunslingers waiting for a striking bell to sound before we reach for our iron. "The finishing your shift part is what I mean. You don't owe me an apology on that count."

I'm still drunk but the time I spent outside with the old lady before waiting out here for Leeson only has me feeling a little tired now. Earlier on, I was up for a fight. Now, I still want to fight but I'm lacking motivation. I'd have to push Leeson into throwing a punch at me or something to snap me out of this sluggish state and get the adrenaline pumping.

He looks to me for a while and finally asks, "What can I do you for?"

"I don't know," I shrug. Silence falls back over us like a thick blanket.

"I was talking about you a little earlier," he says.

"Oh?" I smile. "Talk of the devil," I say, grinning a little wider. "Nothing too serious, I hope?"

"Well," he says and he takes a couple of steps forward but stops, keeping quite the distance between us. "Well," he says again, "I suppose I should be a little glad to find you here. I was going to head over to the Four Card on the way home."

"It must be serious."

"Just a misunderstanding," he says, "I'm sure of it."

"We can always hope," I say to him like I'm making a funny. "But what is it," I ask him, "that's serious enough to have you thinking about me in your place of business?"

"Well," he sigh, slipping his hands into his pockets - trying to have me believe he doesn't want to say what he's about to say but he simply *has* to, "Mitch called me earlier this afternoon. He's a little concerned-"

"Oh?"

"Like I said," he smiles, "I'm sure it's nothing. But Mitch remembered he has some people coming to stay at the motel in the next day or so and that means he needs you to move on sooner than originally thought. In fact," he adds like it embarrasses him a little, "he asked me if I'd be able to encourage you to move on soon."

"Is that all?" I ask. "Mitch says he wants me to go because he needs the room?"

Leeson takes a hand from his pocket and leans against the side of a pew. "Is there something else I should know?"

"I don't know," I sigh, "I don't know. I don't even know if it's my place to tell you this."

"Tell me what?"

I take a deep breath as if in preparation. "Reverend Leeson," I ask him, "have you ever heard the descriptive term of having *an expensive cold*?"

He thinks it over for a second before shaking his head from side to side. "I don't believe I have," he replies.

"Must be a city thing," I shrug. "But an expensive cold," I explain, "refers to users of cocaine, when they've done a little too much and their nose is all blocked-up because of it. This is real difficult for me to say, but I think Mitch is a heavy drug user."

Leeson opens his mouth to say something but thinks better of it; closes his mouth for a moment before deciding what it is he really has to say; "What is it that makes you think that?"

"Well," I tell him, "he can appear a little erratic. Always sniffing," I continue, "can be real nice or real sour… But what convinced me," I tell him like it pains me to do so, "is the undesirables I've seen him meeting. They park outside the motel late at night or early in the morning, Mitch seems to hand something over and takes something in return before they drive on and then he goes back to his room. I tried to ask him about it and he went and bit my head off."

"When was this?"

"They most recently came by to see him early this morning… I'm talking three AM. or around then. I mentioned it when I was heading out for a bite to eat and he wasn't happy. He tried to convince me I was dreaming, so I played along and left. I saw him again a little later," I claim, "only briefly and he was in better spirits, but that was when he started coming out with needing me to move on. But like I said," I say as if to remind him, "I wasn't sure if it was my place to let you know. Whether there is even anything to know," I add.

Leeson nods his head. "Well," he quietly says, "thanks for telling me of your concerns. I'm sure it's nothing like you think, but I'll ask him about it all the same."

"That's good to hear," I smile. "But what can I say? I'm only doing my job."

"Yes," he says, "about that… That gets us back to my original point. Mitch really will need the room back and you have somebody waiting for you up north. Have you spoken with them recently? I only ask because they might be wondering where you are… What's taking you so long?"

"I called them from a diner earlier today. Listen," I tell him, "Mitch really does have nothing to worry about, I'll be moving on in two, three days and I won't leave the place in a mess. All he'll have to worry about," I smile, "is cleaning the sheets and topping up the towels."

"You'll definitely be moving on that soon?"

"Swear to God. Like I said, the plan was always to stay in Whicker for around a week. You and me both know how much can take place over seven days."

Leeson nods his head, pleased at what I've just told him. "I'll let him know," he says, "I'm sure he won't mind as long as you settle your bill and move on with plenty of time to spare before the next guests arrive."

"I'd appreciate that."

Leeson nods again. "Is there anything else you'd like to discuss, or is that everything?"

"There's one thing," I reply, easing the cigarettes and Zippo from my pocket, "but it's nothing too serious. Nothing church-related," I say, placing a cigarette between my lips.

"I'm sorry, but smoking is strictly forbidden inside of the church."

"Of course," I say, taking the cigarette from my mouth and placing it behind my ear. I flick the Zippo open and snap it shut, flick it open again and snap it back shut, holding it just to the side of my hip for Leeson to see. He glances at it for a moment but if the very sight of it means anything at all to him, he keeps it well hidden. "Belonged to my old man," I tell him. "That's what I wanted to talk about with you. You ever think about your parents? You have any thoughts at all about mom and dad?"

Leeson shakes his head from side to side, *No.*

I release a low whistle, like his answer surprised or maybe even impressed me. "Well," I sigh, "I used to think about my older brother from time to time. You know, I always pictured him the way he looked the last time I had saw him. It's funny, isn't it? I mean, if you ever remember a teacher from when you were say four or five years old, you picture them the way they looked way back then. They could have piled on a couple of hundred pounds or maybe even died of old age, but they haven't aged a day or anything like that in your head. They're frozen. Trapped that way for all eternity, am I right?"

"Sure," Leeson reluctantly states, "I can agree with you on that."

"Yeah," I sigh, "I don't picture my brother the way he *used* to look these days. But earlier on," I tell him, "I got to thinking about another important figure from my childhood, my uncle, and not just in the usual way of remembering how bad he could be. I actually thought about him as a man," I smile, "do you understand that? I was wondering if he's a lot smaller than me now, because I always remembered him as being a tall guy. And strong, too. But I was wondering if the years have been far from kind to him… Is he frail-looking? Did all that drinking and smoking kill him off or is he just close to death? You really never think about these things?"

Leeson shakes his head again. "No," he says softly.

"It's funny," I smirk, "there have been a couple of times were I've thought about what I'd do if I saw him again… Wondered if I'd take the advantage if it was there for me to take and give him a kicking. I used to say I'd never return home," I sigh, "but now I'm thinking about how bad it would be if I did. I wonder if he'd recognise me despite being the man I've become. I wonder if I'd feel sorry for him if he was frail, or would anger take control of me? Maybe even fear would take control of me, just for being around him… But you really never think about stuff like that," I ask him, "not even once?"

I hear Leeson's throat click as he swallows. "Not even once," he replies.

"Good for you," I smile. "But I guess it's easier for you," I say, "what with your beautiful family. And they are beautiful… Your wife and daughter, I mean."

Leeson nods. "Thank you," he says. "I've been blessed."

"I don't know about that," I laugh. "I'd say you've been lucky, definitely, but I don't know about *blessed*. I don't know," I sigh, "maybe I'd be able to settle down and find happiness if it wasn't for some things being out of my control. If I could just get what was owed to me, maybe I'd start focusing on the finer things in life."

Leeson clenches his jaw on hearing that; his mood changes right in front of me despite his best efforts to keep it hidden. "You've said that a few times now," he says, "wanting *what is owed*."

"Yeah," I smile, "I have said that, haven't I? Anyway," I say, heading in his direction, "it's out of my hands, it really is. But here's hoping the Lord provides," I say, passing him walking to the exit without looking back. "Thanks for talking with me like this. We should do it again some time."

"You know where you can find me."

"I do now."

I know Mitch has been snooping around the minute I step into my room. He must have thought he was oh so smart, using his key to get in here while I was out, but *everything* is just a millimetre or so out of place. The sheets look a little different from the way they had when I left; where he must have even slipped a hand underneath the mattress in search of contraband. My rucksack has been moved - again, only slightly but enough for me to notice, and I chuckle, picturing his disappointed expression once he had found nothing more than a few clothes and a Bible within. Heaven forbid a travelling reverend carry a change of clothes and a Bible with him; am I right?

Without dropping my smile I make my way to the bed and sit down to kick off my shoes, noticing the white envelope on the floor I had stepped clean over on entering. I get back to my feet and walk over to the envelope. It's pure white and sealed. With it being sealed, I figure it was slipped beneath the door *after* Mitch had spent the day playing detective. I pick it up and sit back down on the bed before opening the envelope. Inside there is a clerical collar (the whitest piece of material I have ever seen before) and a handwritten note from Maria, saying she called by but I wasn't here but she would sure like to see me again and, as promised, she is enclosing one of her dad's spare collars alongside the letter.

I smile and slip the collar into my trouser pocket. I don't know why, I just don't want to wear it yet. Then I think about Maria, and how I could maybe fuck her tomorrow and leave early the next morning without saying a word. Maybe if she stayed the night, I'd see her off at the door the following morning and tell her I'd call her later- only to catch the first train out of Whicker. I don't know, I'd have to make sure I managed to see her before making any solid decisions… Decide what would be a good idea and what was just drunken nastiness coming to the surface.

Bundling the note into a tight ball, I carry it into the bathroom and flush it down the toilet. There's a little dirt on the floor behind the toilet and I can't be sure whether I just haven't noticed it before now or if it's another sign of Mitch's intrusion, like he was looking behind the toilet for stashed goods. "Asshole," I mutter before lighting a cigarette. I sit back on the bed; slip my shoes back on and head out the door with plans of calling for Jack.

"Doyle," Mitch calls me from the doorway of room one. He's smoking one of those cheap cigars of his. He must have spotted me coming back and lit it up right away, maybe building up the courage to pay me a visit but now he doesn't have to because I can go to him.

"Mitch," I say back to him with a patronising wave and a smile.

"In here," he says, heading back into his room, "we need to talk."

He waits just behind the door so he can close it behind me, making sure nobody will disturb us. "Take a seat," he says and I take the same seat I was in just hours ago. I hear him walking behind me and wonder if he's going to attack me but he doesn't. He makes his way to his own chair and sits down. The top buttons of his shirt are unfastened again and the hair on his chest is damp. "What am I going to do with you?" he sighs.

"Move me into the Presidential Suite?" I smile. He doesn't smile back at me.

"This is a good town," he says.

"Sure," I nod. "It's homely, isn't it?"

"I talked with Leeson a little earlier."

"I know."

"No," he says, "I spoke with him *after* you saw him at the church."

"Right," I smirk. "He come rushing over here or did he call you on the telephone the minute I was out of that church of his?"

"He told me you're planning on leaving in the next couple of days."

"Well," I sigh, "that isn't written in stone. I could be persuaded to stay a day or so more, and one or two people would sure like me to stay around for a little while longer."

Mitch swallows and takes a drag on his cigar before slipping a chubby hand into one of his tight pockets. "What if somebody persuaded you to leave tonight?" he asks, pulling a creased and beaten envelope from his pocket. It isn't white and new like the one Maria used, it's brown and old-looking. "Here," he says, tossing the envelope onto the table standing between us.

"What's this?" I ask with a smile, eyes staying on him as I lean closer to the table. I hold the envelope in place with one hand and use the other to iron the creases out, easing my hand from one end of the envelope to the other.

"Open it up," he says as thick smoke leaves his small mouth, "and find out."

"It must be pretty spectacular if you think it's enough for you to bribe me into leaving town in a hurry. What is it," I ask, "pictures of Eliza Dushku or Katy Perry without any clothes? That'd be more than enough for me to leave tonight," I tell him, "and they don't have to be showing their pink assholes or spreading their legs wide open,,, Just give me genuine pictures that nobody else will ever see. Give me pictures only I will ever admire."

"It's-"

"Failing that," I interrupt, "give me an English rose. Give me Gemma Arterton or Kate Beckinsale," I smirk. I don't open the envelope. I don't even look at it. I keep my eyes on Mitch as I continue to push the creases out of the paper. "And how about Emma Watson," I add, "she sure is sweet, don't you think? Looks young and healthy… Reminds me of somebody I know in town."

"There's a cheque in there," he says. "My life savings. More than enough for you to get far from here. Even live the good life for a while if you choose to. Or use it to get drunk and walk out into oncoming traffic or overdose, I don't care which. But go on," he challenges me, "open it up and take a look. You could be richer than you've ever been before."

I stop working the creases out and pick the envelope up off

the table. "I've been plenty rich before," I tell him, "and they say a rich man can't enter Heaven," I add tossing the envelope in his direction like the very feel of it offends me. "Now if you don't mind," I say, getting to my feet and heading for the door, "I've got places to go and people to see."

"Wait!" he barks at me. "I'm not done yet."

I stand there with my back to him and I don't say a word. He asked me to wait so that's exactly what I do.

"I don't know who you are," he says, "or where you've been… No idea the kind of people you've been dealing with. But you know something? You have to say the same thing about me. You think you've had it tough in the past? Well… I can show you just how much worse things can be. I can make your worst nightmare look like paradise, do you hear me?"

"I hear you," I answer, "but I still don't care."

I open the door but he chirps up again before I can step out of it. "You think you got nothing to lose? I can tell Leeson," he says, "and he can look into you. If you're lying about being a reverend… well, do you know if there are laws against that? Do you want to find out?"

"You can tell Leeson anything you want. As a matter of fact," I sigh, "you tell him I'll be at Velma's until late."

"You come back here," he cries as I walk out of the room so I can go visit my good friend Jack, "you don't know the kind of people I know!"

45

Jack opens the door to me and his pupils are wild and he looks a little edgy. There's *no smell* of grass coming from inside his room and that only has me think he's taken something else so, understandably, I want to know *what* and *how*. I mean, when I discussed getting a little blow, he said he didn't have any on him and he couldn't risk getting any for fear of certain people getting to find out where he's been hiding. So has he gone and blown his cover in search of a high or did he just happen to track down a dealer who had no idea who he is or where he was from? It's possible. I mean, Doyle was good at finding whatever he wanted, whenever he wanted it. It was like he had a sense for it or something.

"Doyle," he says with a grin. I see the well-chewed ball of gum near the back of his mouth as he asks, "What are you up to?"

"Depends," I answer. "You want to head over to Velma's?"

"Who's Velma?"

"Velma's," I smirk. "It's the bar we went to."

"Oh," he nods, "sure, sure. Just let me put on my shoes. Come on in a minute," he says and I follow him in so he can sit down and slip into his sneakers. The iPod or whatever he uses for listening to music? A slim set of headphones are connected to it like he was listening to something or was intending to before I disturbed his day. "What've you been up to, anyway?"

"I'll tell you later," I say with a grin. At the back of my mind, I take to worrying about how much of his money he has thrown on recreational drugs today because I was hoping he'd be buying all of the drinks again but I try and shrug it off. I probably have just about enough left in my own wallet to get reasonably loaded, especially if I'm leaving soon and without settling the motel bill. But maybe I could try getting away with using Sam's tab over at Velma's again?

"Man of mystery," he says as he takes to lacing his second

shoe. "Hey," he asks, "you spoken with the chubby fucker who runs this dump?"

"Mitch? Sure," I say. "Why do you ask?"

"He wants me out," Jack grumbles.

"Let me guess," I say, "somebody has booked the room so they can go to a business conference?"

"What?" he smirks, standing up now he's fastened his laces. "Asshole didn't even feed me that bullshit," he says, "just told me he wants me out. Says I'm making the place untidy… like this place could look any worse!"

"What'd you say?"

"Tossed him a little extra money," Jack says like he can't believe it himself, "told him I'll make tracks on the weekend. Fuck knows where I'll be heading. Shit," he smirks, "where's the dog-collar? You look naked without it."

"Lost it," I chuckle. "I've got a new one but I haven't tried it on yet. Wait until I tell you *how* I got the new one."

"I'm intrigued," he grins. "But let's go. We'll have somebody at the store call us a cab."

We head outside and Jack closes the door but he doesn't bother locking it. "You've left the door unlocked," I tell him.

"Fuck if I care," he shrugs on taking out his cigarettes. "Everything I have in there can be replaced easily enough. Fucking let some kids sneak in and trash the place; it'll justify the extra money I handed that Mitch asshole."

Jack buys the first beers once we arrive at Velma's and I tell him everything that's happened since I last saw him; how I got fresh with Leeson's daughter and threatened Pennington's asshole of a son. He laughs, shakes his head from side to side and finally sighs. "But what about you," I ask, still curious to whether he's been out and scored, "what have you been up to? I noticed your car has been gone a couple of times."

"Nothing as interesting as you," he smirks. "Just been looking around and driving through the country… you know how it is."

"You find anything interesting?"

"Well," he grins, "I noticed a lot of the schoolgirls in town are hot. You fuck the reverend's daughter," he says, "you make sure you introduce her to me, first. I won't try and steal her from you," he smirks, "I just want to know what she looks like in case I end up hearing her squealing on the other side of the wall!"

"Hardly any chance of that," I joke, "I haven't had any in a long time. She'll be lucky if she gets more than a couple of minutes out of me."

"She's young," Jack says, "tell her it's supposed to be that quick. Anyway," he adds, getting to his feet, "I'm just using the restroom," and he walks away with me silently wondering if he's off to powder his nose in secret.

46

THE HOURS ARE going by pretty quickly but they always will when somebody else is buying the drinks. Jack says he's going the toilet and then the bar. He gets up and walks away, hand dipping into a trouser pocket. There's no doubt at all he's snorting a little coke each and every time he goes the bathroom now but I don't mention it to him because who am I to challenge what he wants to be kept secret?

"It's all that time wearing the dog-collar," I drunkenly mutter to myself, smiling like it's the wittiest remark ever made. "It has you thinking you're a real preacher."

I finish what is left of my beer and decide I have the time to head outside for a smoke while I'm waiting for Jack to return. His cigarettes are out on the table so I pick them up just to make sure they don't go walkabout if they're left unattended. Velma's is pretty empty so if *anybody* took them it would be the bar staff but even bar staff can claim ignorance when you ask where your cigarettes have disappeared to.

Outside, all is still and quiet. Even the cars on the road go by one at a time, the speedometer reading *Slow Motion*. One will pass and the next one won't appear for a minute or so. Rush hour in Whicker. I finally remember why it is I'm standing outside and light one of Jack's smokes. Breathing tar and various poisons into my body, I wonder what the electronic ones are like and if I should switch to them, if only for a little while. Don't get me wrong, I'm not scared of dying or anything like that, but I'd hate to have an illness like cancer. It eats away at you, leaves you as thin and as weak as wet paper. Dementia is something I'd like to avoid, too. One of my grandparents had that before she died. I don't really remember it too much because I was so young at the time, but I remember how it turned her into a completely different person. She could be rude and aggressive; traits she had *never* displayed before. She also went from smoking near sixty a day to not smoking at all, and that's something seeing how she had apparently taken up the habit a year or so after she was out of her diapers.

I take one last pull on my cigarette and toss it away. Turning to head back inside. I stop, noticing Leeson walking in from the distance like a ghostly apparition. And I smile because I know I'm the one that's called him here so I light another cigarette and wait for him. It's the least I can do.

47

Playing it *real* *cool* I take a drag on my cigarette while slipping my free hand into my pocket. It just happens to be the pocket where I've been keeping the dog-collar Maria gave me, so I smile and gently finger it. It feels soft and new. As fresh as the morning air.

Leeson finally gets close enough to come to a stop. "Doyle," he says. Well, it's more of a tired-sounding sigh.

"Leeson," I say back to him with a nod. "This your local watering hole?"

He looks to Velma's like he needs to be sure of where it is he's standing, regardless of the fact he obviously came here looking for me. "I try not to drink too much," he says, looking back at me.

"A lot of people *try* that," I smirk, "but they aren't so successful."

Leeson asks, "You one of them?" and it has me wonder if that's his first punch or whether I've simply taken his comment the wrong way.

"Well," I smile, "I swiped a bottle of communion wine or two when I was a kid and refilled them with blackcurrant juice and it's all been downhill from there."

Leeson nods and keeps something of a blank expression on his face but his eyes are holding so much more behind them. "I spoke with Mitch," he says, "came here hoping I'd find you as soon as I left him."

"You're in luck," I say. Itching for an act of aggression, I drop my cigarette and step down on it before slipping my other hand out from my pocket. "What is it you want to see me for?"

"I want you gone," he bluntly admits. "Whicker is a good town."

"Yeah," I nod, "I count a total of two people that haven't been very welcoming and that's all."

"It's for your own good you leave now," he says. "Leave before people turn against you and chase you out… Or worse."

"Tell me," I chuckle, "is this you telling me to pack-up and get out of Dodge?"

"I guess it is."

"At least you're honest," I snort. "What did Mitch have to tell you to get you out here like this?"

"Not a lot," he sighs. "You see," he says, "I looked into Saint Claire's, Los Angeles, and couldn't find it. Found an old school going by the name," he adds, "but that was all. Then Mitch happened to call me again to let me know of his concerns. He thinks you're the one with the drug problem."

"He would say that," I smirk.

"Well anyway," Leeson goes on, "I decided to make a few calls and not only is there no Saint Claire's Church in Los Angeles, not one reverend or father out there had ever heard of you before now."

"I try to keep myself to myself."

"You're a snake-oil salesman," Leeson says without any hint of emotion, "a conman out to get anything he can and I won't let you use these people or damage the name of the church any more than you already have done."

"You told the law your theory?"

"It isn't a theory," he says, "and I haven't told anybody… yet. I'm giving you the chance to move on before anybody has to be told what I know."

"You don't mind if I pull this at any other town but here?"

"I'm hoping you'll see how close you came to getting caught out here and give up the act."

"You hope I'll see the light," I laugh, "is that it? And what about *your* act?"

"I don't have one," he says.

"Maybe you believe that nowadays, maybe you don't. I can't say it interests me too much either way."

"Listen," he says, "I've said what I had to say. It's down to you whether you're smart enough to listen to it or not," and then he turns to leave.

"You know what you do have?" I ask him. "You have a

wonderful family."

He stops and turns to face me. "Are you threatening me?"

"No," I reply, "just offering a compliment."

"I'm giving you a chance to leave here before any real trouble begins," Leeson warns me. "I don't want you to look back on this chance and regret how you didn't take it."

"Is that so?" I ask.

"Leave town," he says. "I want you gone tonight."

"How does Laura put up with you? Look at you," I laugh, "playing the tough guy before you go back home and try to convince yourself everything is as it should be; the dutiful housewife you ignore and the daughter you want everybody to see as a little girl because that's how you see her. You got all the lucky breaks when you skipped home, didn't you? You went and got yourself two beautiful girls while I-"

The camel's back finally breaks. Leeson shoves me back before throwing a left I just about manage to duck under. I throw a right and he ducks it before coming up to punch me in the jaw. The blow hurts like you wouldn't believe and causes something inside of me to panic. I quickly throw a punch out of little more than desperation but he's fast. He's under it and back up in no time at all, giving me no room whatsoever to prepare for the second punch he lands. I'm off balance and he takes full advantage of it, landing another punch to put me on my rear. He takes a tight hold of my shirt to lift me off the floor and I taste blood at the back of my mouth. He brings his face up close to mine and I notice how it's now bright red for rage. The idea of sinking my teeth deep into his nose comes to mind but I cast it aside and start laughing instead.

"I'll call Mitch later tonight," he growls, "and he is going to tell me you've gone. If he doesn't," he hisses, "if he doesn't, everything that follows is on your own head."

"I broke you," I sneer, still laughing. "I broke you, brother. See the cut on your knuckles? That'll leave a scar and every time you notice it, you'll remember this moment. You'll remember how I drove you to this!" I laugh but it was all so easy I get no real joy from it. I thought it would make me feel so much better.

But still, I'm not done… Not yet. Not by a long shot.

Leeson releases me from his grip and gives me a final shove just for good measure. "Yeah," he says, "don't make me regret having to do something worse." he pants, walking away. He doesn't stop to look back.

I GET BACK onto my feet and dust myself off. A part of my back hurts a little where I must have fallen at an awkward angle and my tongue manages to find a tooth that feels a little loose but it's no big deal. I light another of Jack's cigarettes, drag the smoke deep inside of me and look over at Velma's. Nobody saw what just happened. "Always the way," I mutter and I decide to head back to the Four Card instead of returning to the bar. I figure Jack will understand when I explain it to him. Some places, especially in the bigger cities, refuse to serve you if you're all beaten up. That's never sat right with me because it's when you've taken a punch or two that you really need a drink.

I get a lot of funny looks on my walk back to the motel. Nobody asks if I need any help and they don't cross the street once they're nearing me but I see them taking as discreet a look as they can manage. If the dog-collar in my pocket was around my neck, they'd probably be falling over one another in a desperate bid to help me. I'm kind of glad the collar is in my pocket because of that.

Back at my room, I head straight for the bathroom to get a proper look at my face. There's a small nick between my eyebrows, already scabbed over, and a purplish-tinge beneath my right eye. My bottom lip is a little puffy, too, but I'm getting used to it looking like that anyway. There's a streak of dry blood running from my lip, across my cheek, where I must have wiped a hand over my mouth without realising. "Nothing broken," I say, filling the sink with hot water to splash over my face. "Nothing broken," I sigh, "nothing gained."

I have a quick wash before looking outside to see if Jack is back yet but can't tell either way. Wondering if Leeson is feeling sore or mad about what I had him do to me, I kick off my shoes and get onto the bed.

Doyle stands at a street corner and gives one of his street

sermons as I lean on a nearby wall and smoke a cigarette. He's not having much luck with the pedestrians; they pass by like they can't see or hear him. He takes to speaking much louder but that only has people speed up the pace to get away from him a little quicker. A man with silver hair parks his car at the kerb and comes walking towards the store where I'm standing, dropping a crumpled dollar bill at Doyle's feet as he does so. Doyle needs all of one second to thank the man and then he's preaching again. To most people, it would seem like he never stopped with his sermon. The older man gets a little closer and stops, noticing me. He asks, "Don't I know you?"

"No," I tell him, "I don't think so."

The man stares at me for a while. His lips twitch into a smile and his eyebrows raise a millimetre or two. "Lee," he says with a wry grin. "It is Lee, isn't it?"

I don't know what to say. The older man does.

"What're you doing back here?" he asks me, drowning out Doyle's golden way with words.

I ask him, "What do you mean?"

"I mean," the old man says, "what're you doing back *here*?"

All of a sudden I realise how I'm back in Sinclair and the old man's identity is no longer a mystery to me. He's Eleanor Gayle's father and it leaves me speechless.

"Have you come back home to see your uncle?"

I wake with a start. It's late or early depending on how you look at it. The room is aglow with the light of the TV screen, the volume down low so you can't hear anything that is being said onscreen. I try to remember if I got up at one point to turn it on but I'm pretty sure I didn't. Rubbing brittle stones of sleep from my eyes, I wonder if Mitch let himself in and turned on the TV in a bid to unsettle me. "Asshole," I mumble, heading into the bathroom. Blinding light stings my eyes the second after I've pulled down on the chord.

49

I TAKE A handful of small stones and toss them one at a time at Maria Leeson's bedroom window. There's a chill in the air that cuts me down to the bone and I'm a little nervous that a light will come on behind the glass window of her parents' bedroom but it doesn't. A curtain is eventually pulled back and I see Maria looking down at me. She looks sleepy but also kinda spectral in the moonlight. She raises a hand in silent gesture before disappearing from view and I make my way to the front door. I wait a while, start wondering if maybe she has fallen back to sleep, but then I hear the locks sliding back and the door inches open just enough for Maria to step outside. "What're you doing here?" she asks in an excited whisper. She's wearing a baggy T-shirt, a pair of cotton trousers favoured by morons who view jogging as a decent way to spend their free time and a pair of black socks.

"I had to see you," I say, stepping forward to plant a gentle kiss upon her lips before taking a step back to stroke her face with an open hand.

"You're freezing cold," she giggles, still to notice my puffy lip or the small cut and bruise around my eyes.

"You offering to warm me up?"

"You're a bad man, Reverend Doyle," she takes great delight in saying.

"How bad?"

"Very bad," she says, moving forward to place her lips upon mine before suddenly pulling away and looking back over her shoulder. "You hear that?" she asks.

"No," I reply, blood pounding inside of my ears.

"Fuck," she mutters, "it sounded like one of the floorboards had been stepped on. Do me a favour," she says, "and wait around the side of the house."

She closes the door on me and disappears. I smile, take the

cigarettes and Zippo from my pocket, head to the side of the house and light up. And I just stand there for a while, smoking my cigarette and wondering how long I've been waiting here… Wondering if she did hear something or whether it was only in her head. Finally, she steps into sight and heads in my direction with a nervous smile on her lips. "Well?" I ask, pulling her close.

"It was nothing," she says and as I hug her I look over the windows of her neighbour's house and wonder if somebody in hiding is watching us. More than anything, I *want* somebody to see us outside like this. "That's my weak-spot," she tells me as I take to kissing her neck.

"That's good to know," I say, dropping the cigarette to my feet while I continue to kiss her throat, the cold air losing its bite as I do. I get excited at the thought of Leeson or his wife finding it here in the next couple of hours and wondering where exactly it came from. It excites me but that isn't the reason behind my fat one.

"Wait," Maria says as she excitedly pulls herself away, "I've got something to tell you."

"Oh?"

"Mom and dad were fighting," she says. "It was about you."

"Me?"

"Yeah," she says. "I didn't hear much, just your name. And dad told me to stay away from you. What's happened?"

"I don't know," I tell her, playing dumb. "Do you remember what exactly was said?"

Maria shrugs her shoulders and looks away for a second or two. "Let me think," she says. "Dad came home and I heard him banging around in the bathroom and then he came into my room to ask if I had seen you at all."

"And what did you say to that?"

"I told him how you came by the house to speak with mom and he said he wasn't talking about that and he wanted to know if you'd been back here or if I had seen you at all since then. I said I hadn't and he said that was good, and that I was to keep away from you and he would be angry if he found out I was lying to him. He told me I wasn't to even talk to you if I saw you in the street and then he stormed out of my room and went downstairs to have an argument with mom in the kitchen."

"And you heard my name being mentioned?"

"Yes," she says, "I think. He'd slammed my door shut so I didn't want to open it, in case it made him mad," she smiles. "I put my ear to the floor to try and listen but it didn't do much good."

"Forget about it," I smile, kissing her first on the lips and then on the chin. "We've got nothing to worry about," I tell her. I kiss her throat and bend my legs at the knee, kissing the material of her T-shirt that keeps my lips from her subtle breasts. I kiss lower and lower, Maria breathing heavily as I get down on my knees and lift her shirt a little so I can kiss her warm and flat stomach.

"That tickles," she says.

I continue to kiss her stomach but gently tug at her sweatpants and panties, easing them down just below her hips and around her thighs. I get my first glance at her beaver. It's as cute as hell but could do with a little trim. The hair reminds me of a scrubbing brush. I just about manage to dab the *right spot* with my tongue and my reward is a brief acknowledgement of that salty-sweet taste before Maria cups a hand beneath my chin and pulls me up as she eases her underwear and trousers up with her free hand. Her eyes are still closed. I kiss her on the lips hoping she will taste herself on me and when we separate, she opens her eyes and looks at me before smiling. "You're a bad man," she says, softly tapping my chin with one of her fingers as she says every single word.

"I'm the kind of man your mother warned you about," I whisper and it makes her chuckle.

"I have to go back inside," she says. The expression on her face makes me think just saying those few words hurt her.

"You want me to come with you?"

"Yes," she grins, "but you can't."

I kiss her on the lips and then once more on the forehead. "Come see me tonight."

"Where?"

"The Four Card. Come by and we'll have a drink and listen to some music."

Maria smiles, "What kind of music?"

"I don't know," I shrug, "how about The Brian Jonestown Massacre? You ever listen to them?"

"No," she says.

"Then we'll listen to them. Just turn up around eight o'clock. Tell your parents you'll be staying at a friend's house to do some homework or something like that."

"What about Mitch?"

"You want me to invite Mitch?" I joke before returning my lips to hers.

"No," she chuckles. "What if he sees me?"

"He won't," I tell her, "just trust me. But what do you say," I ask "are you going to come over?"

She smiles. "I don't know if I can…"

"Sure you can," I say, kissing her while slipping a hand underneath her T-shirt and planting it atop of firm breast.

"Your hands are so cold," she grins.

"What do you say?"

"Okay," she smiles, "I'll come by for eight o'clock. But now I have to get back inside," she adds, pulling my hand out from under her shirt. We kiss one last time and as we separate, a thin strand of saliva runs from my lips to hers.

50

I WAKE WITH a start, hearing the whine of a mosquito close to my ear but I can't see the little fucker. The little vampire falls silent so I slap at the side of my head and roll out of bed, surveying the walls and even blankets in case it landed nearby. I give up on trying to locate it, wonder if I was maybe dreaming and then head into the bathroom to rid myself of my morning wood. I think of Maria. I think of the noise she could make if she has never had sex before tonight and so the responsibility of opening her lands on me. And if she *has* had sex before?

I smirk. Guys around her age with scrawny peckers. They might have put it up her but I'll still be the one who broke her in.

Just one flush of the handle and my potential descendents are swallowed by water and sent down one pipe after another. I fix my trousers and take a quick look at myself in the mirror. The bruise around my eye doesn't look any better or worse. What had been a small cut between my eyebrows now looks no worse than a pimple but my lip could easily go unnoticed.

Reaching for the cigarettes in my pocket, I remember they're Jack's and decide to pay him a visit to let him know of the latest developments (and ask if I could borrow his iPod and whatever for that night while doing so…) so I light up and head outside. His ride is there but he doesn't answer the door no matter how hard I pound my open hand against it. "Fuck," I say. Admitting defeat I take a retreating step to head back into my own room and notice a sign up in the window of room one, Mitch's room, so I walk closer to it and get a good look. It says:

SORRY! BUSINESS TO SEE TO - CLOSED FOR DAY.

There's a cellphone number underneath the message but I don't pay much attention to that. Instead I look around to be sure nobody is watching and then I try opening the door but it won't budge. I put a little effort into it, just in case it sticks, but it's no use. Mitch has gone out for the day and locked up good and proper. Before my arrival, he probably didn't feel the need to ever do that. I try to let go of the disappointment I feel on being kept out of his office like this by trying to convince myself how there'd probably be nothing of interest in there anyway. I mean, even if I forced my way in to look around for the cheque he had offered me, he could cancel that in no time at all. Maybe even have me arrested for trying to cash it, depending on what story he has to tell.

BUSINESS TO SEE TO - CLOSED FOR THE DAY.

I take a drag on my cigarette and just stare at the sign for a minute, wondering if there could possibly be some truth in his claims of new guests due to arrive any day now. I could imagine Mitch running out for new towels and fabric softener to impress a bunch of yuppies.

"Yuppies," I mutter under my breath, "I've always hated them," and I slip a hand inside of my pocket and smile, feeling the soft and smooth touch of the collar that sweet Maria had lifted just for me. Thinking about her, I try Jack's door again but he still doesn't answer and I'm left wondering if he's ignoring me, like he's sore for how I left without saying a word to him. It's possible, especially if he *was* snorting blow last night. I'm not trying to preach here or portray myself as being whiter than white, but the most selfish people you can meet are those who are a little too reliant on coke. And if they're somehow not selfish then they're assholes desperate to be worshipped. Think about it, practically every major actor or failed actor or major singer/songwriter or failed singer/songwriter dabbles with it. Me? I only ever touch the stuff for recreational purposes.

I bang at Jack's door again, a little louder than before. "Jack," I call through the thick wood. I knock at the window and try to look within but the curtains force me to remain on the outside. "Fuck it," I say, just loud enough for him to hear if he's listening from behind the door. "Fuck it," I say a little louder, walking away in a sour mood with no real idea to where I'm headed. I kick a stone and watch it bounce and skip across the asphalt like it's trying to lead me into a local grocery store, so that's exactly where I head, the automatic doors sliding open for me once I'm near enough for them to detect me. I aimlessly wander the aisles for a little while and Doyle comes to mind so I focus my attention like a laser on the collection of newspapers and glossy magazines to try and forget about him before I take to feeling a little blue.

Sharon Osbourne is featured on the cover of one of the magazines and I don't read the headline but instead realise how the woman doesn't even have to open the stiff lips of her Halloween-mask-like face to piss me off. Spotting those little scrotums known as One Direction on another magazine, I turn to walk away and remember how Maria is due to visit me tonight so I head to the counter to buy a cheap bottle of wine and ten cigarettes with most of the money I still have to my name.

"Bag?" the clerk asks despite how he's already bagging my items for me.

"Please," I say with a nod.

"Anything else?"

I look back at him to say *No* but happen to notice packets of condoms on display behind him. I consider pricing them up but drop the idea, realising how I could probably get away with telling Maria I'll just pull out of her when the moment comes. She's bound to be clean and even if I knock her up, it's not like I'll still be around to have to deal with the consequences.

51

THE DAY CRAWLS by and not at a snail's pace but a sloth's. I don't see Jack despite how many times I knock at his door. He doesn't leave, he doesn't make a sound, and I take to wondering whether he's real angry at me for leaving him in Velma's or whether he's sleeping off a hangover or dead from an overdose or something like that. I'm a little pissed at him whatever his reason because without his iPod and those speakers he can attach to it, I won't be able to play any music around Maria. I figure she'll have to do with whatever happens to be on the TV in the background… Congratulations, Maria, every time you hear the Deal or No Deal theme tune, you'll remember the night your cherry was popped.

At around ten minutes after eight I open the bottle of wine and take a mouthful or two. After another ten minutes I just start drinking it properly. With only half the bottle remaining, I take to wondering just where exactly Maria is and what she could be doing, standing me up like this. I smoke one cigarette after another while gently fingering the collar that's still in my pocket to try and slow down my drinking but the bottle is eventually finished. Annoyed, I get to my feet and angrily step outside. I look up and down the street but can't see her coming.

"Little bitch."

I pull my shoes on and head outside, closing the door behind me but not locking it. The light isn't on behind Jack's window so there's clearly no point in knocking at his door again so I decide to head for the Leeson family home with no idea to what I'll do once I arrive there. Noticing a flyer pushed underneath one of the windshield wipers of Jack's car, I drunkenly pull the folded paper free and crumple it up before stuffing it into my pocket as I walk along. Venturing onwards, I light a cigarette and keep walking, trying to stay in a straight line so I won't look too drunk. A blue or black van passes and parks up just ahead of me. As I'm about to pass it, the side-panel door rushes open but I think nothing of it. Somebody says, "That's him" or maybe it's even "Are you *sure* that's him?"

I'm not too sure about what's said but I turn to see two guys rushing out. It's not a good look, I don't pick up any facial features or scars or anything like that, just the fact that one of them is holding a baseball bat. The bat is pulled back and then swung with some force, connecting with the side of my skull. I lose consciousness for a fraction of a second; regain it right after the back of my head crashes into the sidewalk. I'm dizzy, unable to move and it feels like I'm about to barf.

"Get him in," another voice quickly says, "get him in!"

The two that jumped out of the side of the van take hold of an arm each, pull me up off the ground and push me into the back of the van. It's even darker in the back of the van than it is on the street and I can smell motor oil. The floor seems damp and sticky and I wonder if it's spilled oil or my own spilled blood that's responsible.

The van rocks a little as my attackers jump back inside and pull the door shut. "Drive," one of them says, "drive!"

The engine growls and the van starts moving. The vibrations of a quick exit from the street we were on shakes through the body of the van and into my own.

"Is he unconscious?" somebody asks. I'm already struggling to keep a count of how many guys there are in here with me.

"His eyes are open."

"That doesn't mean shit. See if he's unconscious."

"Hey," a voice I've already heard says as somebody gets to my side and rolls me onto my back, "you with us?"

I can't see his face, just his outline against the darkness. He holds the flame of a cheap lighter near my face. "Shit," he says before permitting the flame to die, "I think we've brain-damaged him or something."

"I didn't hit him *that* hard," a disembodied voice sneers. "He's just out for the count, that's all."

We keep driving for a long time. I stay on my back throughout the journey, occasionally bouncing a millimetre or so off the ground when the van goes over a speed-bump or something. Saliva runs from the corner of my mouth and down my cheek until it eventually slips into my ear canal but I don't try to wipe any of it away. I'm increasingly becoming aware of my surroundings but my body may as well be a slab of iron for all the control I have over it right now.

"I'm telling you," somebody whispers from the darkness, "we've completely fucked him up."

"Well what did you think we were going to do to him?" comes the silenced reply.

The vehicle moves on for what feels like days. Over the time, I become all the more conscious and my thoughts continue to become clearer and clearer but I may as well be in control of another body entirely, one thousand miles away from here for all the use mine is to me. And I wonder if they could have paralysed me. I've never understood people saying they can't feel their legs or something after a terrible accident because I can't say I'm always so aware of mine, and the feeling of the sticky floor on my face and hands doesn't comfort me so much, just in case I'm now a cripple from the waist down or something. I think the term is *paraplegic*.

"This'll do," somebody says. The van comes to a stop. I hear the side-panel door sliding open and then the two men who ambushed me, the same two that have kept me company during the ride take a hold of my arms again and pull me out without grace. My legs are of no use at all and I'm only kept standing by how I have an arm around a man at either side of me. Even my head is slumped forward so I can't get a good luck of where I am. It looks like we're on a lonely stretch of highway but we could be absolutely anywhere. The darkness stops me from getting a good luck at the man at either side of me or the man standing in front of me... the driver, I'm guessing. I hear somebody sneeze from inside the van and it blows my mind, it really does. The fact somebody can sneeze at a time like this, like what's going on is completely natural and not at all out of the ordinary?

"Hey," the man in front of me says, "are you awake?" He starts clicking his fingers in front of my face, takes my chin in his hand and lifts it so I have to look in his direction but my head flops back towards my chest the moment he releases me. "Hey," he asks a little louder, "are you awake?"

"He's awake," the guy to my left says.

The guy in front says, "You know what this is about, don't you? Sure you do," he sneers, leaning out of sight for a second just to collect the baseball bat or whatever it was used against my skull from the back of the van. "You know what this is about," he insists.

A puff of flame seems to appear as of nowhere while he lights a cigarette and I wonder if I've just blacked out for a moment.

"You were warned," the guy in front of me says, "you were warned," and then he forces the bat into my stomach and I nearly double over but the other two keep me up. Panting for breath and in agony, I'm a little relieved because at least I know I haven't been crippled. Not yet, anyway.

The handle of the bat is brought crashing into my jaw. The world spins around me. If it wasn't for the two keeping me down, I'd float off into the cosmos and never find my way back. The guy backhands me across the face and I taste blood. The two men keeping hold of me offer words of encouragement to their friend. I'm hit time and time again. Eventually the guy dishing out the beating slams his forehead into my nose and I know it has just been broken for the second time in my life. The two men responsible for holding me up drop me to the road. Maybe the sight of all the blood rushing from my nose had them decide I'd had enough already, maybe the broken nose was the signature card of the man now wielding the bat.

A foot kisses my ribs with passion.

"Fucker," one of them says and I hear him spit but whether it was at me or not, I can't tell you. They all climb back inside the van without offering another word. Doors shut and an engine starts. Face down on the asphalt, I watch the lights of the van as they move off into the distance, eventually disappearing altogether.

52

I CAN JUST about make out the dust on the road in front of me that moves forward every time I breathe out through my open mouth. The taste of blood on my tongue is thick and heavy. I can feel the blood on my face drying in the cold air and I worry about it drying so hard it sticks me to the road for all of time.

With more than a little difficulty, I roll onto my back. The moon is full and so bright it hurts to look at. I can see a lot of stars shining alongside it, plus a thin section of cloud that looks to stretch for miles, twisting here and there so it looks like a giant snake making its way across the heavens, devouring eternity. Something howls way off into the distance and an ice-cold wind rushes along the surface of the road and chills me right to the bone. I shiver, or at least I hope it's the cold making me shiver and not a sign my body is about to quit.

"No," I mutter, "it's not that," and I know it's not that because I can feel my heart beating strongly inside of me. Stronger than I ever knew it could.

The stars flicker like they're trying to communicate using Morse code or something. Stars my friend Doyle would say we were from and would return to on dying. Just thinking about him causes me to move my tongue over my teeth. They're all there, right where they should be. Give me a busted nose over missing teeth any day of the week.

I take a deep breath and struggle to exhale for some unknown reason and it scares me. I feel my heart take to beating a hell of a lot faster before it slows down again but the big problem is how it won't stop slowing down… My heart is quitting on me, I can feel it.

The stars continue to sparkle, continue to offer me a chair among them. And I smile, realising I have no reason to refuse - not any more.

I slip a hand into my pocket figuring I'll have one last cigarette before dying but find the dog-collar Maria had given me instead. It looks almost silver in the moonlight; the once brilliantly white collar now stained with my blood. With trembling and clumsy fingers, I attach it to my throat with difficulty.

The blinding light of twin stars, temporarily earthbound, comes rushing towards me from the horizon with plans of taking me back with them. I think of Leeson and the name I knew him by long ago. I think of how I beat him and his new life and how his town can never be the same again because of it. I was the serpent in his garden.

I take a deep breath and feel my heart stop beating the moment I close my eyes and smile.

53

IT TURNS OUT the great hereafter is little more than lying on a small, rickety bed in a box room with yellow wallpaper and a worn navy blue carpet.

No, this isn't Heaven or Hell. It isn't Purgatory, neither, I realise. No almighty being would go to such trouble with Earth and the universe before deciding *this* would do just fine as the afterlife.

My ribs hurt like hell as I force myself into a sitting position. For the first time I notice the bedside table to the right of me whilst also realising how I'm seeing the world through eyes half-closed due to the bruising caused by a recently busted nose. I open the top drawer to find the few clothes I have left neatly folded and tucked away in there. My shoes are in the drawer beneath.

"Where am I?" I mutter.

There's a framed photograph on the wall. After staring at it for a couple of seconds, I realise I've seen it before; it's sepia-toned and shows a small boy being photobombed by Jesus. Quite a gag for the son of God to pull and way ahead of its time.

I reach into the top drawer again and rummage around for the cigarettes I had on me but they're gone. My Zippo lighter is still inside my trouser pocket. I'd have thought that would have been first to disappear, not an almost finished packet of smokes.

I swing my legs around to the floor and the pain in my sides is so bad that my breath is stolen from me. I notice my ribs are bandaged up and wonder how I didn't notice earlier, what with the material being pulled so tightly against my skin. Getting dressed is a gargantuan effort because my whole body takes to aching. The dog-collar underneath my black shirt isn't the one Maria had given me. I know this because there are no bloody fingerprints staining it *and* this one feels old and a little used. The torn beer mat is still tucked inside one of my shoes. I smile, seeing that.

I open the door and wonder if I was wrong and that this *is* the afterlife, because all I see is an open corridor with the same yellow wallpaper and the same worn carpet. Closed doors, plain wood, not varnished and without a number or letter run along each side of the corridor.

A lighter but no cigarettes. This has *got* to be Hell…

I clear my throat and get walking, taking slow and easy steps that don't make a sound, and sigh when reaching the end of the corridor and spotting a descending stairway. I make my way down the stairs, passing framed paintings of Christ and the blessed Virgin before reaching ground level and pushing another plain door open. All I see is a couple of chairs and a bookshelf hiding an entire wall.

"Oh," I hear a woman say in surprise. I turn to where the noise had come from, spot a sister or a nun standing at yet another open door. She's young and beautiful; too much of both to be wearing a habit and carrying so much responsibility. "You're awake," she says, smiling as she straightens her posture to gather herself. Despite how friendly she is, I can't help but feel a little troubled at finding myself in front of a woman of religion. I mean, if she asks, do I introduce myself as Reverend Doyle or Father Doyle? One is bound to mean a lot more than the other as far as she is concerned.

"Where am I?" I ask but even now, trying to decide in advance whether I'm Father Doyle or Reverend Doyle seems more important to me than asking how I got to be wherever I'm at.

"The Missionaries of Charity" she says like that explains everything and to most people, it probably does. "You were brought here only yesterday. It appears that you were hit by a car that left you in the middle of the road. Terrible, isn't it? Still," she smiles, "you don't look to have been knocked about too badly."

I hear footsteps moving directly above me, look to the ceiling and then back to the sister. Or nun. Whatever she is.

"One of our residents," she smiles. "Almost time for them to leave," she says, "but they'll be back tonight if there is room. It's a shame we don't have the space for every unfortunate we try to accommodate."

"Yes," I nod because I'm guessing it's the expected response. "I was hit by a car?"

"That's what we were told. Do you not remember?"

"A little. How'd I get here?"

"Somebody found you and brought you here. A doctor examined you. Your nose was broken but that was the worst of it. The rest is just bruising."

I nod as if in understanding, look to the floor and then back at her. Her eyes dart up from the same piece of carpet I'd just been looking at and focus back on mine. "My cigarettes?"

"Oh," she smiles, "we don't allow smoking or drinking here. I'll return them to you whenever you're ready to sit outside."

I nod again and bring a hand to my throat. "This isn't my collar."

"No," she says, "Father Adrian was kind enough to give you that. Your collar… Well," she sighs, "it was a little dirty."

"Where am I?"

She looks at me like maybe I've asked her a trick question. "The Missionaries of Charity," she responds.

"No," I smile, "where am I? I was hitchhiking from a town called Whicker."

"Oh," she blushes, "I am sorry! You're in Tryfords," she says. "Where is it you're travelling to?" she asks.

I open my mouth to talk but no words come.

To be concluded in
"Every Open Eye"